# Ram With Red Horns

# *Ram With Red Horns*

# Rhys Davies

Introduced by Philippa Davies

seren

**seren** is the book imprint of
Poetry Wales Press Ltd
Wyndham Street, Bridgend,
Mid Glamorgan, CF31 1EF
Wales



A CIP record for this book is available at the
British Library Cataloguing in Publication Data Office

ISBN: 1-85411-165-5



*Published with the financial support of the*
*Rhys Davies Trust*

Printed in Plantin
by WBC Book Manufacturers, Bridgend

# Introduction

With over a hundred short stories, seventeen novels, an autobiography, a musical, a play, topographical and historical writing to his credit, Rhys Davies is easily the most prolific of Welsh authors who write in the English language. It is curious therefore that in the 1990s his work needs to be reintroduced to the reading public.

The dictates of fashion and the cultural dichotomy within Wales exemplified best perhaps in the insistence of such central Welsh language literary figures as Saunders Lewis that there is no such thing as Anglo-Welsh writing, have not been helpful. Neither had Davies' long, self-imposed exile: he left Wales in the early 1920s returning only when his precarious financial position deemed it necessary. At such times he would cloister himself at his parents' home, write furiously until he could secure an advance from a publisher and return speedily to London where he lived most of his adult life. There he was a prominent member of the avant-garde, Bloomsbury set which included such literary figures as H.E. Bates, Liam O'Flaherty and Hugh McDiarmid. Among this circle of acquaintances, his sexual ambivalence was accepted and his personal freedoms not curtailed.

Davies was also not the kind of person who wore his Welshness conspicuously. Welshness, he felt, is not a worthwhile concern in literature and in the quest for success, compatriot writers should '.... stop thinking of themselves as Welsh ...' and '... consort as much as possible, with people who dislike Wales, or, better still, are indifferent to her'. Such sentiments would not have endeared him to the Welsh literary establishment. The effect of this physical and emotional distancing from Wales was such that, when his autobiography, *Print of a Hare's Foot* was published in 1969, many thought he was dead. The situation continued thus for the remainder of his life: in 1976 when he was awarded the Welsh Arts Council principal prize, he failed to collect it. Recent years have, however, seen the beginning of a justifiable revival of interest in his work. A biography is being compiled, an anthology of short stories is to be published and television and radio are showing interest with several dramatisations of stories being broadcast. The posthumous publication of *Ram With Red Horns*, his last novel, is the latest in this series of initiatives.

Davies was born in Blaenclydach, half way up the Rhondda Fawr Valley in one of the tributary cwms rising steeply above Tonypandy. During his youth he described it as a place of contradiction, 'rough and well behaved, religious and drunken' but despite its 'fidgety population and battles for economic reform' it was never as radical as the 'little Moscows' of the coalfield. Through boyhood eyes there appears to have been little that was grim about the place other than 'wages and God'. His parents, whose roots were in West Wales, kept the rather grandly named Royal Stores, a grocer's shop situated in the main street and opened in the last years of Victoria's reign. Other local landmarks included a large red-brick pub, the Central, which features often in his writing, and also the Cambrian Combine, owned by D.A. Thomas, Liberal MP for Merthyr and then Cardiff, later to become Viscount Rhondda in Lloyd George's war-time government. Advanced cost-cutting methods at the Cambrian ensured frequent strikes, the most bitter and protracted of which precipitated the legendary Tonypandy riots of 1910 during which a large number of shops were wrecked and looted. There was also fierce hand-to-hand fighting between police and rioters. Blaenclydach remained quiet for some time during the troubles but later had its fair share of battles. Royal Stores was spared: Davies' father was sympathetic to the miners, he allowed credit and as a man of standing in the community, helped less literate customers with their correspondence and legal affairs. Umbilically linked with the fortunes of coal, the business flourished during the years of prosperity which marked the early twentieth century, a situation which was to be dramatically reversed in the 20s and 30s as debts incurred by striking miners families mounted. Early prosperity meant that the family belonged to the comfortable if not affluent middle class. They could afford a servant and also a horse and trap, which, Davies remarked, '...made them appear stylishly well off in comparison with nearly all the shop's customers'. His mother, an uncertificated primary school teacher before her marriage, was the dominant partner. It was she who kept a controlling eye on the business, chastising her husband for allowing too much credit and '...swooping drastically' on customers when untidy ways were suspected. She had, however, a deep respect for colliers' wives and for their husband's struggles for better conditions. There can be little doubt that it was she who inspired the numerous energetic but invariably defeated women who, in later years, peopled her son's writing.

As a child, Davies attended the local primary school and then moved on to Porth County School. Not particularly academic or well motivated, he found school dull and repetitive, finding more pleasure helping with menial tasks around the shop. Later, when older, he was allowed to deputise for his father, debt collecting and taking weekly orders from well established customers. The latter, he recalled, was more in the nature of social visiting and took place when the day shift men had returned from work. The insights he gained at this time were a particular source of inspiration for his early work. His apathy towards education led to a sudden departure from Porth school. His parents suggested a number of 'respectable' careers: journalism, local government and banking. He rejected all and, after a period of inactivity during which he read voraciously at the local miners' library, he took up employment at a men's outfitters in Barry. The purchase of a pair of spats and a silver-topped malacca stick were hopeful symbols of freedom and symbols also of an ever widening gulf between himself and his contemporaries: those from the middle class embarking on careers in the professions and those from miners' families already working in the pits. From Barry he moved to Cardiff and then on to London where he continued in the outfitters business, a pre-literary career pattern which exactly matches that of Caradoc Evans, Davies' nearest contemporary within the Anglo-Welsh literary genre. On dreary Sunday afternoons he wrote a number of short stories which were accepted by a periodical entitled *The New Coterie.* In 1927 his first novel, *The Withered Root,* was published and from then on he was able to support himself solely from his writing. In those days, he reminds us, 'shoe-string living needed little money'. During the inter-war period he travelled frequently and extensively in Europe and in 1928 on one of these trips he met D.H. Lawrence. The friendship prospered until Lawrence's death in 1930, the older man casting a critical eye on the fledgling author's efforts and becoming an important, living literary influence. In terms of literary achievement Davies may be regarded as a writer of serious but also humorous fiction. During his lifetime his work was well received both in Britain and in the USA. His short stories were particularly popular and have been favourably compared with those of Chekhov and Maupassant. After a short illness he died in London at the age of seventy-seven.

Apart from his prolific output one of the defining characteristics of Davies' work is its essential Welshness: his first ten novels and the majority of his short stories are set in Wales and while his primary concern is the universal experience of the individual the landscape of his imagination is indisputably Welsh. This is a curious fact bearing in mind his calculated outsiderdom. There is another factor, however, which makes Davies a considerable literary figure: within the Anglo-Welsh tradition he is the first realist writer. With the publication of *The Withered Root* the genre took a new course. Life is presented not as it might be, more picturesque, more adventurous and more heroic, as is the case in the novels of earlier writers such as Allen Raine, but as average and commonplace. Characters are people who are not remarkable in any way and they live through ordinary experiences of childhood, adolescence, marriage, parenthood and old age unexceptionally. Life is often dull and sometimes unhappy though it may be brightened occasionally. The introduction of this tradition of writing into Anglo-Welsh fiction was radically innovative and in the truest sense Davies was a pioneer. He was, however not a socialist realist as was his contemporary, another Blaenclydach born novelist, Lewis Jones, author during his short lifetime of two novels, *Cwmardy* and *We Live*. The essential dynamic of society for Davies is not the struggle between classes but the struggle of the individual for self-determination. It is in the exploration of this concept that Davies, like Lawrence before him, emphasises the power of the unconscious to affect human behaviour.

Translated into abstract, thematic terms, much of his work is the working out of Davies' personal philosophy of individualism but there are a number of supporting themes. The most significant of these by far is the constrained position of women in early and mid-twentieth century society. In his industrial novels, this translates into an illustration of material deprivation, prematurely deteriorating health, domestic violence and lack of opportunity both economic, social and personal. This is shown to affect women of both the working and middle classes, albeit in a different way: material comfort, as many of his impoverished women characters are duped into believing, does not guarantee personal fulfilment. Davies, then, offers an oblique perspective on his native region, one which is a far cry from the matriarchal society of conventional mythology popularised best in Richard Llywellyn's *How Green Was My Valley*.

This interest in and concern with the woman's lot is continued in those novels set in rural Wales and in this context *Ram With Red Horns* is no exception. Davies' last novel, it is set in an unspecific, small-town setting in West Wales during the 1960s. It is a tale of female vengeance enacted against a social background of declining nonconformist influence and the rise of political nationalism. Continually dreaming of a red-horned ram seen first on an outing to a local beauty spot Rhonwen is reminded of past unhappiness. The ram returns again and again to haunt her sleeping hours and becomes a potent metaphor for what she regards as her husband Adda's sexual excesses and indiscretions. Her means of confronting and dealing with this recurring nightmare represents the central theme of the novel. As is invariably the case in Davies' imaginary world this struggle is painfully realised but necessary in the quest for laying to rest the spectres of the past. Eirene, Adda's mistress, is the second central figure in the novel and, like Rhonwen, she is similarly tormented by a vision of the ram. As both women are drawn into a struggle to reconcile the real with the ideal a close and unlikely bond develops. In her lack of inhibition and rejection of conventional mores Eirene bears striking resemblance to several other of Davies' heroines. Most notable among these are Blodwen of *Count Your Blessings* and Cassie of *Jubilee Blues*.

The social and political context of the novel affords the opportunity to explore and reflect on the parochialism of small town life. Bedd Einon, as the name implies, is unremarkable and decaying. However, supposed links with the glories of a legendary

Welsh past fuel and perpetuate a pretentiousness comically and vividly embodied in such local institutions as the High Class Family Butcher, the bustling Women's Guild and in Paris House, the grandly named draper's shop. Nationalism and the burgeoning Welsh consciousness of the period are also alluded to. In their anti-intellectualism and anti-Englishness, Mrs Pyle-Williams and Madoc Howells represent the less attractive face of the Welsh nationalist movement. Dewi the poet's blind and unquestioning adherence to the ancient poetic traditions of the past compounds this sense and further illuminates Davies' unease with the political and cultural climate of 1960s Wales.

As *Ram With Red Horns* and most of his literary output implies, Rhys Davies is a person of great contradiction. He claimed not to be a sociological writer yet the social aspects of life are everywhere in his work; he claimed to be politically detached yet is vigorous in his attack on social injustice and double standards; he denied his nationality yet the greater part of his work is set in Wales. In the *Story of Wales* he writes of the effects on the national consciousness of centuries of English cultural and political domination.

> Chains are curious things. They can be made to vanish while still about one, they can blossom like the pilgrims staff. But for England, ... insensitive though she often is to the claims of the Principality Wales to-day might be a wistful orphan whose ancestry is wrapped in obscurity. Instead, occasionally reminded of the fact by the clank of chains, there is a nation stoutly and firmly aware of itself ...

In this passage Davies could well be speaking of the effects of his own long, self-imposed exile. Surrounded by much that was foreign he too was reminded of his ancestry and this brought forth a body of work which in its literary context is unique in its perspective, challenging in its insights and radically innovative in both form and subject matter. It is for these reasons that he occupies a unique position among his contemporaries.

— Philippa Davies, May 1996

# One

On the fine day when Rhonwen achieved the deed of becoming a widow, a year or so after she had made some awful discoveries, she prepared a steak and mushroom pie in the morning, in readiness for her and Adda's evening meal. Today she baked with it a quick currant-dotted cake known by the native name of *teisen lap*. A perfectionist, she weighed all ingredients on a pair of Victorian shopkeeper's brass scales of which she was very fond, polishing it and a row of weights frequently, and even playing shop with it, weighing cereals and dried fruits from her larder canisters into paper bags.

That afternoon, following a cold lunch, she and Adda were taking the car on one of their trips to Pen Mawr, a lonely headland commanding the best view of an imposingly wide bay, its coastline unscarred by human developments, the Atlantic sometimes demurely blue and smooth, sometimes blackly seething, springing despotically over savage rocks far below the cliffs, exactly as such water had behaved since the beginning of things. From Pen Mawr Adda intended to set out, after the picnic tea, on his usual seven-mile walk along the coastline, returning home by bus. Now nearing sixty, he was proud of his undiminished stamina and orderly body.

He had retired from his job as head accounts clerk on the Gas Board three years before. He decided to retire early, instead of waiting until he was sixty-five, because of an inheritance of thirty thousand pounds from his father, plus shrewdness with his own investments. There was also the prompting of a philosophy of self-indulgence. He wanted to enjoy his life while the going was good. Since his retirement he had talked of taking Rhonwen — really it was her idea — on a long sea cruise, its main point a visit to their married daughter in Australia. The expensive trip was to be a kind of winding-up celebration of their term as man and wife. Yet he had done nothing to put the venture into practice, and Rhonwen now thought she knew the reason for his procrastination. That he had long become pathologically cheese-paring at home was a tributary reason, comparatively trivial.

Since her important discoveries of his perfidy, she had begun to see him as a sly, reddishly yellow tom-cat with an existence completely of his own. He became a stranger, except that there were sacred links with the distant past, now desecrated. This vision had originated in a dream that, like others afflicting her, was vivid because of the kind of sleeping tablet she now took every night. Dreams were colourless, except for a uniform greyness, yet a sense of that lurid reddish-yellow came through, and the cat could have been a fox. All the dreams seemed to open deep wells in her. She would suddenly swim up to the wakened plane in palpitating horror, a stranger lying beside her in the inherited bed of carved black oak. Was she the same woman who had married this shifty person, irregularly snoring, beside her? He too sometimes had restless nights, including muttering in his sleep. His excellent body was not entirely master of his mind.

Besides retaining the symmetry of his figure, Adda had a bushily vigorous ginger moustache. With his hat of locally-made tweed, its brim jauntily turned down, his well-cut suits of similar fine tweed, he strode about in self-contained assurance, gait not delayed or abridged by haunted thoughts, a wholesome country gent esteemed at the branch of his bank in Bedd and, with some reservations (when alcohol kindled tongues), at the Bowling Club pavilion. In addition to taking those long walks on the coastline, he exercised daily with a skipping rope and an old pair of dumb-bells. Altogether he was a man who made the phrase 'in the prime of his life' apposite, somewhat past its season though he was in calendar years. He had, however, long ceased indulgences with Rhonwen.

She had preserved, at fifty-three, some of her baby-face attributes, especially in her soft, rose-tinted complexion and large innocent-seeming blue eyes. Lately those eyes had become a little pendulous and red-rimmed; they fixed on people with a suggestion of hard criticism, taking everything in, rather disturbing to those susceptible to such scrutiny, a sense of guilt being so common in people. Slight but tenacious, her soft padding footsteps were definite and purposeful. Orally, she did not ramble or waste time, and her voice had been of some musical consequence in her day. It slurred over nothing and she never shouted. Altogether she knew how to maintain a self-respecting aspect and a recognition of the decencies in the parish of Bedd, where she and Adda were born. He referred to her so frequently in the Bowling Club and elsewhere as 'a good wife' that it seemed to be the praise of a man requiring to convince himself or to veil something unworthy in his own conduct. She could easily have been nicknamed Rhonwen the Good Wife locally.

Their house, called Cartref, was hers, inherited from her parents, and in her will, drawn up a dozen years before, ownership of it would pass to Adda and, at his death, to Marged, their Australia-settled daughter. Adda's separate will, made at the same time, bestowed all his money on his wife and, at her death, the residue to the daughter, who probably would have become a more devoted letter-writer had she known of these arrangements. Marged had always itched to leave home and indeed Wales. But Rhonwen was proud of her; she admired large decisions and drastic measures. The prolonged delay over the expensive sea cruise to Australia had much rankled.

They set out for the trip to Pen Mawr at two o'clock. On the way there, or back, Rhonwen wished to gather a load of blackberries, in a scrubland where the fruit was lusciously big if the summer weather had been favourable. Adda was very fond of bramble jelly and she usually potted a couple of dozen of the preserve — for her own enjoyment too, of course. 'You are going to drive or me?' she asked, as Adda opened the garage doors. She liked driving and was the better driver. But Adda thought it unseemly for her to drive when they went out together, and had seldom yielded. 'I,' he replied curtly. 'What do you want that walking stick for?' It was a stick that had belonged to her beloved father, a thick ash with a curved silver-banded handle, suitable for a sturdy countryman's grasp. She had taken it once before, recently, on this trip.

'Alma Thomas was bitten last year by a snake sliding from under a bush. She — '

'I've got a letter to post. Demand for the rates came last week. Gone up again.' Adda had been occupied in the morning at his writing bureau, which he always kept locked, even from his wife, who, as secretary and treasurer of the Women's Guild in Bedd, had a desk of her own, also a separate bank account.

'Alma was taken to hospital and — '

'What do they do with their rates money?' Adda placed the picnic hamper on the back seat.

Rhonwen, closing the garage doors after he had backed out, did not betray her annoyance. Adda's recent maddening habit of interrupting her when she opened her mouth, going off on subjects of his own, grated on her out of all proportion. She had noticed that it was not only with herself that he showed such bad manners; it was as if nobody impinged on him except as a pair of ears. Sitting beside him in the car, she looked at his hands on the wheel. They clenched very tightly, the knuckles white. Yet there had been no indication of bad temper that day.

Both were drivers of many years' experience. When Adda had used the car for the eight miles to the Gas Board offices in Melin, Rhonwen had wanted a small runabout of her own; they could afford it. But even then he had displayed the parsimony which, since he had retired, increased in so many petty ways, such as an insistence on low-watt electricity bulbs and, earlier this year, going to cheaper accommodation for their usual spring week in Devon, with another week in October. After the time when Rhonwen thought she discovered the true reason for all his stinginess she had bought two high-watt bulbs for the living room in Cartref, declaring that her eyesight was being ruined, but when she had gone to bed Adda had replaced them with the weak ones, and she had let the matter remain at that, silent.

'I intend to live until I'm ninety,' he would say, out of pride in his body. He leapt with the skipping rope on the front lawn, stood tensely upright with the dumb-bells and bent to touch his toes, his sinewy behind towards Cartref, at a window of which she sometimes stood, wishing she had a bow and arrow. She had never given the bumptious villain a full-scale dressing-down; she was not that kind of woman, those pale eyes never blazing.

'Want me to help pick the blackberries?' he asked as they descended the thornbush-fringed lane from their hillside house above Bedd village. The offer could have come from realisation of his brusqueness a minute ago, on a picnic day.

'I can pick all I want myself on the way back,' she decided.

He liked to start without delay from Pen Mawr for his long walk along the coast, taking a stroller's path winding in and out. He returned home by the six-thirty bus from Dulais, a small fishing town on an estuary. It was the last bus — there were only three a day serving the route which took in Bedd and proceeded to busy Melin. Rhonwen would drive home and be there in plenty of time to prepare victuals for the famished walker. He sometimes boasted of the walk in the Einion Arms at Bedd, his physique evidence of its health-giving properties, his heart as sound as all his investments. A pint of ale, taken in separate halves, was his allowance in the Einion, where he never bought anyone a drink, earning respect thereby.

'We can go next week for more,' he grunted. 'Ripen for three weeks up there.'

'I don't think I'll make so many pots of bramble jelly this year.'

'Why?' He had listened fully for once, connecting with his favourite jelly.

'The price of sugar. I wonder you don't consider that.'

'Make the jelly less sweet.'

'I like it sweet.'

'Make half of the pots sweet, half sharp,' he pointed out, the Gas Board accounts manager to the fore.

'I'll see,' she murmured vaguely.

The foolish conversation petered out, as had so many others, their abrasive undercurrent seldom emphatic. In the village centre Rhonwen waved to a fellow-member of the Women's Guild, who had stepped out of Iorwerth Roberts', High Class Family Butcher, crossing the road to John Jones' drapery shop, called Paris House, situated between a healthy branch of Barclays Bank and the Einion Arms, a pub of bleak exterior.

Bedd Einion, its full name, is beautiful in its setting and plain-faced as a village, its stone dwellings, shops and three Nonconformist chapels puritanically matter-of-fact, and even its ancient St Dyfed church of workaday aspect. Its slapdash extent, much enlarged since the days before it earned a dot and name on maps, has no charming design. But it is fringed by an azure trout stream among russet boulders, and high on an inner cleft of the vale is a lacy waterfall, which is an example of the genetic loveliness frequent in the county. Bedd, as usually it is called, also has one or two claims on the legendary. Situated on an eminence is a cairn of loose flat stones, under it the remains of a warrior of Owen Glendower's insurgents, whose name had become Einion in the talkative course of time (Bedd meaning sepulchre). Roving back much further, to brutal pre-Roman times, is a Druidical myth relating to a roughly-hewn monolith standing upright in what is now a field where corn grows. Of Amazon height and girth, and curiously swollen in the middle, the stone's upper section resembles a torso and head, its lower a pair of legs. Tradition relates that it is a vestal priestess who had sinfully yielded up her chastity and as she crossed the field to meet her lover, perhaps to discuss her condition, she was turned to stone by avenging gods. An English academic from Aberystwyth University College, who owned a holiday cottage in Bedd, once gave an afternoon talk to the Women's Guild and favoured another less popular version — that she was sacrificed at the spot by priests and the stone was carved and erected as a warning. Poppies flourish in the fields and of course their red is associated with the woman's blood.

'I forgot milk for the thermos tea,' Rhonwen suddenly remembered, before they were out of the shopping area. She went into the Co-operative stores opposite the shabby War Memorial, dated 1920 and, as stated on the plinth, unveiled by Lady Charlotte Prys of Careg Castle. When she returned with a half pint in a plastic container, Dan Evans, Insurance Agent, was chatting to Adda through the car window.

Insurance Evans raised his cap to the wife of one of his numerous clients and remarked it was just the day for blackberry-picking and Adda's strenuous walk. 'I wish I could tramp like him,' he said, 'and get rid of this tub of tripes.' He patted his extreme stomach. 'Bending at bowls is getting to be a strain . . . See you in the Club on Saturday, Adda.' The Bowling Club had a seven-day licence for intoxicants, and really it was more that than the beautifully-kept lawn that maintained it as a profitable all-male sanctuary, now that some up-to-date women patronized Bedd's three pubs, which closed all day on Sundays.

After inattentively saying 'Eh?' and Dan repeating himself, Adda answered curtly, 'Hope to be there.'

'Adda's not been well, Dan,' Rhonwen said in a low voice, still on the kerb as her husband started the engine. 'Sleeping badly. The walk to Dulais will do him good. Something on his mind, I think.'

Adda's disposition was known to be erratic. Once he had assaulted a fellow-member at the Bowling Club, and the two men had to be separated by scandalized others. Most people thought he ought not to have retired from the Gas Board before his time. Nobody criticized Rhonwen for being the cause of blemishes in her husband's character. She was quiet, her demeanour, speech, movements and manners inoffensive, her ancestry highly esteemed. Her term as treasurer of the Women's Guild was renewed every year, though Mrs Pyle-Williams, the president, tended for some reason to be a little offhand with her. But then, Mrs Pyle-Williams could be as prickly as Adda and had even found the Aberystwyth professor objectionable, besides being English. She took strong exception to his lecture on Bedd's local monuments, considering it to be disparaging, and had avoided sitting next to him at the ensuing tea-party, with its home-made cakes and hot buttered pikelets. 'I heard the true story of the priestess from my grand-parents,' she declared afterwards, in her obstinate way, 'and I told it to my children, and they'll tell theirs. The Druid priestess never had her throat cut in the field. I trust the story as it has come down to us over many hundreds of years. The priestess is there.' Mrs Pyle-Williams was wealthy, a Nationalist and member of Plaid Cymru. She had been married twice, both husbands frail but well-off, and malicious people hinted that she hastened them to the grave with her demanding bossiness.

'Why did you bark like that at Insurance Evans, Adda?'

'Bark?'

'Sometimes your voice gives people a blow on the nose.'

'I want to get on with my walk. Evans gossips like an old woman.'

They were silent for several miles. As they passed through the outskirts of Melin, the sizeable county town where the Gas Board had its offices, Adda reduced speed as if wishing to linger among his old haunts. Melin had lost much of its ancient character, but with its weekly market for farm and other produce and, on a separate day, for cattle, it is still important. The main street glistened with new shop frontages; there were two supermarkets and, in the Town Hall, a magistrates' court where the shoplifting these establishments encourage was punished with very minor fines — in the weekly local newspaper the offenders took a greater punishment from publicity. There were seven Nonconformist chapels of various denominations, now much less flourishing, though the one called Horeb is famous for its annual week-long singing festival which, since a committee of business men and a charted accountant took charge of it from the chapel deacons, shows a substantial profit instead of a substantial loss. Soloists well known in Wales and elsewhere were ready to appear in oratorio performed in renowned and commodious Horeb.

There was no necessity for Adda to drive through Camber Road, a tree-lined street of late Edwardian houses built in pairs, though certainly it avoided the busy shopping street Rhonwen always liked to see, as he knew. 'Why are you going this way?' she asked, mildly enough, betraying nothing.

'Less traffic.' One would have thought Melin was London or Manchester.

Sideways, she watched him carefully. Sure enough, as the car slowed down, half way through the street, he turned his head to look at a certain house on his right — one as unexceptional and well-kept as its neighbours, bay windows on ground and upper floor, with decent curtains and panes clean, small front garden tidy, a monkey-puzzle tree in its centre. No person looked out of the windows. In a second or two Adda increased speed to the permitted thirty. Rhonwen's face still betrayed nothing. She stared ahead, hands quiet on her lap, claw-thin fingers clasped.

'If we came to live in Melin,' she said, 'this is a street I would choose. It's — '

'Never liked Insurance Evans. Nosy. Pity he's the only insurance agent in Bedd.'

She repeated her remark in a louder and firm tone, adding 'Melin's got conveniences.'

'Live in Melin? Why?'

'The shops and the market and a cinema.'

'I worked here over thirty-five years. Seen enough of it.'

'Have you?'

'You can take the car most days now and drive here yourself.'

'There's old age to think of, and a good hospital here,' she pursued, in this conversation-making way, 'and there's bad winter days to think of.' Only last winter Bedd had again been cut off for days by a monster fall of snow, a not extraordinary event. Bedd residents survived such onslaughts of nature without disaster. At least the vale was sheltered from the fury of the Atlantic gales, the sea an attacking force in which a ship was lost now and again.

The subject of a move to Melin had not been broached before. Adda half-glanced at his wife. Was there something the matter with her? She had always been given to her own kind of secrecy, but suddenly gave vent to thoughts or wishes that might have preoccupied her for a long time; such as abruptly deciding not to sing in the Choral Society any more. Even he had noticed a detachment in her manner since he had kept postponing that promised cruise.

'Shall I pick the blackberries with you?' They would soon be reaching the low-lying sheltered glades where the brambles flourished.

'I told you before — no. I'll pick all I want on my way back.'

Only one car, going the opposite way, passed them on a rough steep road of no consequence except to a couple of small farms and the few persons wanting to reach Pen Mawr, mostly walking enthusiasts from England ferreting out these byways in August. In one or two fields below the farms, sheep looked up from their munching to stare at the intruding car, especially a monster-horned ram glowering near a gate. Their breed was known to be arrogant and even ferocious, but they produced the most tenderly succulent lamb and mutton in Wales, and the renovated old wool mill on the bank of the soft-water stream gurgling outside Melin benefited from their dense coats, the products of tweed and blankets lasting twice a buyer's biblical life, excepting corruption by moth.

'That one looked a nasty ram,' Rhonwen observed. Bred in deep country though she was, she did not like walking through a field of the local sheep, yet she did not mind cows. These livid-eyed sheep could suddenly develop mob-hysteria and gallop with hostile speed, for no reason known to human beings.

Precipices, assertive black rocks and sombre mountains lay far up the vale. Nearby were the centuries-old dry stone walls enclosing such pasturage as remained up here. In a few minutes they reached the coast, where there is no road, only a beaten track over which the car gently bumped. The sea air, on this balmy September day, was deliciously fresh. Yet, as Rhonwen had hoped, nobody else was taking advantage of the autumnal serenity up here. Clumps of gorse bushes, writhing landwards, fringed the cliffs and patches of coarse grass around.

Pen Mawr was a hump of cliff rising higher than the rest of the coastline. There were no beaches in the bay; the sea dashed over rocks far below or, in tidal retreat, exposed narrow stretches of shingle. The Dulais estuary, with its fishing village a little way inland, lay off the bay's curve on the right. Adda's walk there would take him over two hours. The sea today was placid, and no boat could be seen. A few gulls welcomed the visitors' arrival, perhaps aware there would be a picnic meal, with crumbs thrown, as was often the case on fine Sundays in summer, though seldom on weekdays.

Adda fetched the hamper from the car. Rhonwen carried a rug, the carton of milk and, for some reason, her father's walking stick. She spread the rug on a flat patch near the verge of the cliff, and opened the hamper without delay. While she unpacked, Adda, who had a good head for heights, stood at the verge admiring the view and, as usual, taking deep breaths of the air, his back to her, a single tenacious gorse bush beside him; she had known him bring his skipping rope here and take fifty counted leaps. On her knees, she crawled two yards towards him. Rapidly she hooked the curved handle of the walking stick around his left ankle, tugged with a force surprising in so frail-looking a woman, and was successful in the swift trickiness of unhooking the handle. He went over with a yelp of moderate strength. Another cry was lost in the screams of gulls flying from their habitations and perches below. Circumstances that day had proved to be in her favour, with opportunity coming quicker than she expected.

Quickly too she replaced in the hamper the few objects she had taken out and bore it to the car. She snatched up the rug and stick, threw them on the passenger's front seat, got in on the other side, slammed the door with the same decisiveness, backed the car and turned. The whole operation since their arrival had taken less than ten minutes.

She drove rapidly, with complete disregard of the bumpy track; she bounced up and down like a young girl celebrating great news. Exultation possessed her such as had not been hers since the birth of her child, who, despite later indifference to her, had been an achievement she would have liked repeated, especially for a son. Sections of the landscape before and below her became a wild liquescent run of colours, not to be sorted out, yet carrying a surreal harmony of shapes. As the car made a sharp swerve, there seemed to be a collusive wrenching in her mind, a dislodging there, a ripping of senses. Something that was concrete caught her eye, something moving on her right. In a clump of twisted gorse bushes appeared a ram, head thrusting forward as if about to charge and butt. His magnificent horns were red. It was only a momentary glimpse in the distorted gorse, but long enough for his evil eyes to be noticed, protuberant, hostile and vindictive. What was he doing up here? Strayed? Sheep did not come so far from the inland hillsides and fields, though, tumult somewhat curbed by the glimpse, she recalled reading in the local paper that a fully-grown ewe, perhaps elderly-eyed and stupid, had tumbled over the edge of Pen Mawr. Someone in a rowing boat had seen the body on the rocks, gulls swooping on it.

When, after a fifteen minutes' descent and a turn into a by-lane, she reached the blackberry copses, exultation had diminished further. But a freshness still blew through her like a wash of iridescent bubbles, clean and releasing. Her eyes saw more steadily now, the countryside adjusted to its normal lineaments. On a patch of grass, where the straggling lane took another turn, there was a two-seater grey car, empty. Someone else had arrived for blackberries. Ample room remained on the patch for another car or two. Rhonwen got out and, surveying the copses, saw not far in among the tangles of path-intersected bushes, a head wearing a pleated mauve turban. She was pleased.

Myriads of fat blackberries glistened in the lingering sunshine. Wicker basket in hand, she moved slowly in the direction of the woman, picking blackberries here and there, including some reddish ones, which she found added a tang to her jelly. In a few minutes she reached a clearing where the woman stood picking from a circle of bushes crammed with fruit, enough to fill a dozen baskets. The stout woman was about fifty, wore a floral dress and two strings of beads, and smiled in greeting, pleased to find a companion of housewifely demeanour like herself. 'A champion lot this year!' she said.

'That your car I saw? I put mine beside it in the lane.'

'My husband's. Shall be collecting him in Melin at half past five.' The woman's voice had the local intonation, musically up and down. 'I only want enough for a few pots of jam and two plates of tart for tomorrow — my niece and her children are coming.' She carried a foil-lined trug.

Neither had stopped picking blackberries. They established the easy local contact without hesitation. 'I live in Bedd,' Rhonwen provided credentials. 'My husband has set out for a walk from Pen Mawr to Dulais along the cliff tops. Takes Powell's bus home from there.'

'That's a long walk.'

'Does him good. Sleeps better after it. He's been having trouble with his nerves lately.' Rhonwen gave the familiar sigh of connubial endurance. 'Retired from the Gas Board in Melin three years ago and doesn't know what to do with all his time . . . . I make seedless jelly of these,' she added, 'seeds get under my husband's dentures.'

'My husband used to know someone working for the Gas Board. Isaac Thomas. Married the daughter of Matthews the butcher.'

It was to be expected. Nearly always there is some connecting knowledge of families in such towns and villages, more frequently when marriages, births and deaths are concerned. 'I think I've heard Adda mention the name,' Rhonwen said. 'You know Parry Moses?'

'By name. Wasn't his wife a singer?'

'*He* was. I've done a bit of it myself in my time. Sang in the chorus in *Elijah* at the Horeb festival about fifteen years ago. Parry Moses was the best singer I ever heard. Brought tears to my eyes in his solo *It is Enough*. They used to say he ought to go to London and train to be full-time in opera. But . . . well, he went *wrong* privately.'

'Ah,' commented the woman, not really interested in musical affairs, 'some go like that.' Adjacent to each other now, she dropped a very crowded sprig of berries friendlily into Rhonwen's basket. 'His wife, was it?'

'The bottle, I *heard.*'

'My name is Mair Edwards. I live in Mabon Road, leading down to The Old Mill.'

Rhonwen mentioned her own married name and the name of her Bedd house. The other had passed through Bedd many times and knew about Einion's grave and the woman-shaped monolith in the field. The half-hour among nature's bountiful fruit passed in one of those civilized mutual attractions. 'You would like a cup of tea now?' Rhonwen asked. 'There's a picnic hamper in my car. My husband wouldn't wait for tea at Pen Mawr. Wanted to start on his walk. A mania for exercise. He uses dumb-bells every morning, and a skipping rope with painted handles same as in girls' schools . . . . His figure,' she added, somewhat antagonistically, 'is active as a young man's, but I can't say the same of his mind.' She smiled bleakly at the other wife.

'My husband hasn't kept his figure,' Mrs Edwards joined up; 'beer.' She glanced at her watch. 'If I'm late to collect him at the Council Office, he'll be at the pub next door.'

Their receptacles were heaped with lustrous berries. Rhonwen had not fetched a second basket from the car; there would not be need to make as many pots of jelly this year. They strolled back to the cars. Rhonwen fetched the rug and spread it on the grassy verge; Mrs Edwards helped her carry the hamper and sat down comfortably on the ground. Three plastic boxes contained crustless triangular sandwiches, jam tartlets and pieces of *teisen lap*. For the thermos tea there were cups and saucers of fine china, each piece wrapped in tissue paper, matching plates, apostle spoons of gleaming sliver, a jar of lump sugar and large cerise paper napkins. It was no rough-and-ready picnic spread. The guest admired; her hostess was a housewife to be approved.

'Pretty cups and saucers!'

'Belonged to my grandmother. I like good china. I've picked up some nice oddments here and there in antique shops.'

'My husband's got a fancy for one of those old Welsh farmhouse dressers. But he hasn't come across one yet. Not that he looks far.'

'I've got one in my kitchen,' Rhonwen said immediately. 'Adda was saying the other day we ought to get rid of it. He likes modern furniture and I do too. I will tell him you are interested.' For some moments she lapsed into a muse, sipping tea, her jaw, like her eyelids, dropping and looking oddly larger in its grim squareness.

Mrs Edwards gazed in some concern at this small, pensive, friendly woman who was married to a man who sounded a little cranky, with his girl's skipping rope, dumb-bells and long solitary walks.

Rhonwen was thinking rapidly. A golden opportunity had come her way. She opened one of the plastic boxes and said, 'I made this *teisen lap* especially for him when I was preparing a steak and mushroom pie this morning, ready for us when he comes back hungry after his walk. He likes *teisen lap*.' She paused, her face contracted. 'To tell you the truth, he went off in a bad huff, stopping the car before we reached Pen Mawr. That's why there's all this food. I don't know what's been the matter with him lately. It worries me.'

Mrs Edwards, who had accepted a large slice of the cake, which is best eaten on the day of baking, asked, 'Has he been to his doctor?'

'Doctor? He'd think it insulting to his body. He'd have to break a leg before allowing Dr Llewellyn near him, even though they play bowls in the same club.'

'Moody?' Mrs Edwards said, all sympathy.

'He tosses and turns and mutters in his sleep. We've been planning a cruise to Australia to see our married daughter, but he keeps putting it off.'

Mrs Edwards praised, 'You know how to make *teisen lap* for him.'

'Not that he's a *bad* husband, mind you!' Rhonwen bit into the last cucumber sandwich.

'We mustn't worry about them,' Mrs Edwards, who had a hearty appetite, comforted. 'They're just not the same as us.' Accepting a jam tartlet, she asked, tentatively, 'It isn't religion, is it?' When her hostess shook her head, she proceeded, 'Religion doesn't happen so often now. But there's one in our street, coming to him late in his life. He goes on his knees in the back garden to pray out loud, looking at the sky. Neighbours think it's because he was nasty to his wife and it sent her off to Kingdom Come. Their three children won't have anything to do with him.' She dabbed a napkin on her lips. 'Religion takes tighter hold than many things. Still, it's better to have that than heavy drinking or — ' she paused, as if feeling her way to the fit expression, '— loose living.'

'Other women, you mean?'

'There's not much of that in our parts, is there? We're not Cardiff or Swansea, where they can hide it better.'

The repast and gossip concluded, they stowed away their baskets of blackberries. A wasp had begun to buzz above them. Rhonwen invited her guest for a visit to Bedd on a Sunday afternoon. Perhaps Mrs Edwards could bring her husband to meet Adda and take a look at that old kitchen dresser. Mrs Edwards readily accepted; they exchanged addresses on sheets torn from a shopping-pad. Mrs Edwards did not have a telephone, as Rhonwen had. The Sunday after the next one was settled on, unless changed by post.

Their cars were not out of sight of each other all the way to Melin. Mrs Edwards waved a hand when she drew up outside the Council offices; Rhonwen waved back as she went past. Taking the road to Bedd, she knew she had made, if not a friend, at least a well-disposed acquaintance. Not that it was likely the woman would be needed in an important way.

She had carried a transistor radio into the kitchen, where, after washing the picnic crocks, she turned the gas oven indicator to number 3, which would be quite warm enough for heating up the steak and mushroom pie. An alarm clock ticked on a shelf of the dresser. She set its bell for seven; she always liked to time her cooking thus, though her memory was not faulty at all.

There was nothing special in the usual depressing six o'clock radio news, but she waited for the entire fifteen minutes of it to elapse before switching the set off. Then she laid places for two on the living room table, where dusk was gathering. She looked in the silver mustard pot; Adda liked mustard and there was enough left from yesterday's fresh mixing. When she switched the light on at last D his strictures against using current unnecessarily still had force — the cutlery shone and chrysanthemums picked that morning rode sprightly in their vase. She laid two linen napkins in silver rings on the plates beside the cutlery, glanced at an old leather-cased carriage clock on the sideboard, then crossed to the window.

It gave over the front garden, a long view of the village, half a mile below, and a range of mountains above which the day's fair sky had darkened to a greyish purple, but the view did not include the road on which Powell's last bus had travelled from Dulais, due to arrive outside the Einion Arms at five to seven. A ten minutes' walk from there, and Adda would be home. Suddenly she remembered she hadn't lit the rings under the pans of potatoes and carrots, and hastened to the kitchen, though there was plenty of time. Parsley for buttered carrots was already finely chopped.

After gazing meditatively at her pair of gleaming brass scales on the table, she went into the other front room, which was a kind of parlour used mostly when special visitors came, including, in rota, Women's Guild committee meetings which really were gossiping tea-parties. It contained the best furniture, ornaments and pictures in the house, some remaining from her parents' time. She lay on a renovated scrollback sofa, closed her eyes and lapsed into a muse. She saw, as when she had looked it up in an old atlas belonging to Adda, an ungainly sectionally tinted shape. Its pink, yellow and mauve colours ran into each other now, a blurring conveying nothing except that Marged lived somewhere in it, a far-away domain to be reached by devious routes, in great luxury, no expense spared. She was roused sharply from her dream by the peremptory ringing of a bell. The alarm clock! She jumped up, went to the kitchen and turned off the oven gas. The pans of potatoes and carrots were boiling quietly. She took the basket of blackberries into the living room and laid it on the sideboard.

At seven fifteen she telephoned the Einion Arms. Ben Bowen answered. No, Adda hadn't been in. Yes, the bus from Dulais had arrived on time; the driver had brought in a box of hake on order and gone on to Melin as usual. 'Oh, Mr Bowen,' she said, 'Adda went for his walk from Pen Mawr to Dulais and was catching that last bus.' Ben suggested, 'Perhaps he lost it.' She said, 'He's never lost it before.' Ben thought a car could be hired at a Dulais garage and to this unlikely extravagance she replied, 'No, he's walking home, I expect. Mrs Bowen well, is she?'

At eight o'clock, her voice more harassed, she telephoned the police constable's house, which, since Bedd had grown, had a blue lamp marked *Police* over its door in the main street. P.C. Vaughan was out, and she spoke to his wife, Hannah, who was a member of the Women's Guild. Like Ben Bowen, Hannah suggested Adda had lost the bus. 'Oh, I'm *worried*, Hannah!' Rhonwen cried, 'He's not a man to lose a bus. His dinner is spoiling in the oven.' Hannah thought there was nothing else to do but wait longer. Her own husband had gone to a farm about something and ought to be back in an hour on his bike. 'I'll mention your worry to him,' she added dismissively. A baby had begun to wail in the background.

Rhonwen did not touch the pie, drained the vegetables but did not parsley-butter the carrots. She sat with a small glass of sherry and three sweet biscuits in the living room, then jumped up and consulted the local telephone directory. Yes, Powell's Bus Company was in it, a Melin number. Would the office or garage be closed? The company served a large portion of the county, but the Dulais to Melin service was of minor consequence. After a long ringing, a man answered. He seemed unable to absorb the caller's dilemma, kept saying 'What?' then clarified, 'Driver of the Dulais bus has gone home. Can't tell you anything. People get on and off buses. They lose them too.' Rhonwen exclaimed, 'If the driver was the regular one he'd know my husband.' The man said, 'Phone at half past seven sharp in the morning and you might catch the driver here. Goodbye to you now.' It was as if husbands went astray every day.

'I've done all I can,' she told herself, and realized she had not.

At nine she approached the telephone, changed her mind, went to the kitchen and set the oven at Mark 1, to rekindle the odour of the pie. She waited half an hour and found P.C. Vaughan at home. Yes, Hannah had told him of the previous call. Rhonwen's voice rose, 'Oh, I'm so anxious now! Where is he? He's never done such a thing before. Why hasn't he rung me? I've phoned Powell's in Melin and the bus driver has gone home. He'd know . . . . ' Cutting her short, Vaughan said he would come along at once on his bike.

She took him into the living room, where, flanking the vase of glowing chrysanthemums, two places for a long-retarded meal were laid gleamingly on the oval walnut table. A pair of lounge chairs flanked the modernised fireplace. Vaughan, still in uniform, laid his bucket helmet on the hearth rug and stretched his legs from his chair. Born and raised in Bedd, he had served a term in the Welsh Guards, divorced a raffish London girl after two years of her, and returned thankfully to his own people. Hannah always waved his lustrous auburn hair with her own tongs, and altogether he had retained a debonair aspect, his manner a trifle languid. It upset him that he had not yet been granted a car, Bedd not yielding enough return of known improprieties to justify the expense.

Rhonwen did not sit down; she was incapable of settling, and moved from table to window several times. Vaughan listened to some preliminary details, taking out a notebook and ballpen in readiness, if needed at all. ' . . . He stopped the car where I was going to pick those blackberries over there on the sideboard and said he'd walk the rest of the way up to Pen Mawr, where he always did exercises, touching his toes many times and breathing in and out. So I went picking blackberries and met a lady from Melin on the same job, a Mrs Edwards who lives in Mabon Road, and we had a long talk and two cups of tea each from my thermos. She and her husband are coming here Sunday after next to meet Adda and see an old farmhouse dresser I've got in the kitchen. They might buy it if they and Adda agree on a price.'

Vaughan looked patient, fulfilling a routine job, as duty required. 'Perhaps he lost the bus from Dulais.'

Rhonwen's sigh was deep. 'They all say that — Ben Bowen, Hannah, that man in the Melin bus garage and you. But Adda is not here, is he, and it's nearly ten o'clock, his dinner waiting all this time in the oven. Something must have happened to him. If he lost the bus, why hasn't he phoned me?' She went to the window yet again, a hand pressed over the region of her heart.

Thus somewhat reprimanded, Vaughan jotted a few words in his notebook. Rhonwen's agitation in this petty mystery had registered; a wife of long standing could develop a sixth sense where her man was concerned. He asked Adda's age and what he had been wearing, and said, 'Let me phone the Dulais police station and see if they have anything to report.' The enquiry accomplished, he came back from the hall and sat down again. 'No information there.' As if to wean her from too drastic a solution, he related, 'About a year ago there was a Melin case of a married man missing for a whole week. Found in Birmingham. Memory gone.'

This halted Rhonwen in her restless prowling. 'Ah! Is it that? . . . Adda!' she half-whimpered, 'memory gone!'

'Did he have money on him?'

Recalled by the factual enquiry, she replied irritably, 'How could he pay his bus fare without money?'

'Big money, I mean. The man in Birmingham had over a hundred pounds on him. Slept in a tramps' hostel.'

She had sat down at last on a chair pulled out from the pleasingly laid table. 'I don't know how much money he had.' The pale eyes no longer roved. 'Loss of memory! That's what it is.'

'There've been signs of it?' Vaughan asked, his touch of languor returned. He seemed to be restraining a yawn.

'Retirement from the Gas Board hasn't suited him. He misses his ledgers. We made plans to go for a long cruise and stop in Australia to see Marged, our married daughter, and her two children that we've never set eyes on. Adda sent for information from a shipping company months ago. Lately I said to him, 'We must hurry up and go to Australia before we get too old to enjoy the trip", and he said, "What do you want to go to Australia for?" I answered "Marged and her children," and he only said, "Oh!" One would have thought Marged had never been born. His own daughter that lived with us here till she was twenty!'

'*Sounds* like loss of memory.' Vaughan jotted in his notebook and glanced at his watch. 'Anything else?'

She paused for a moment, a loyal wife, and admitted, 'Touchiness; bad-tempered over nothing. He hit a man in the Bowling Club one evening. But never a slave to the bottle, mind you.' Nothing of Adda's gross parsimony was mentioned.

Vaughan ran a hand lightly over his perfect hair-waves. 'He can't be reported missing yet. You will phone the bus driver at seven tomorrow morning?'

She suddenly wailed, 'But Adda must come back before then! He must! He must!' Less distressfully, she said, 'We had booked for a week at Torquay in October. We go there twice a year.'

The only restraint from threatening hysteria Vaughan could offer was 'Hannah asked me to tell you she won't be able to attend the Women's Guild meeting tomorrow. She thinks one of our twins is going to have measles. Off food and nose running. Ought to have had it in the Spring, not now.'

Rhonwen burst out again, perhaps imprudently, 'Am I likely to go to the meeting myself?'

'Your husband might be walking home *now*,' Vaughan remarked, closing his notebook. He was not inexperienced in domestic tantrums, disputes and spites. This couple were mature, but long-buried resentments, if they surfaced at all, could be all the more fierce in ripe people, until the inertia of old age set in. 'He's only about three hours behind time,' he pointed out. 'Not much to go on. I'll wait till the morning before reporting to our Melin station.' He took up his helmet and blew off it a shred of pollen. 'Phone me or Hannah if Adda doesn't turn up and you catch the bus driver.'

At eleven, front and back doors locked and bolted, she cleared the dining table and removed the blackberries to the cool of the kitchen window sill, not favouring placing them in the fridge, since she hoped to cook them next day. She ate some crackers and Caerphilly cheese and went up to bed. The policeman's visit had satisfied her. She had done her duty and he his. She felt no criticism of herself. A power in directive charge of her had taken full possession for the policeman's visit.

The releasing exultation she had felt at Pen Mawr, as she speeded away in the car, returned a little now. But in the bathroom she took two of the sleeping tablets prescribed by Dr Llewellyn, double her allowance. Adda had known nothing of her visit to the doctor over a year before, and had never seen the tablets, the prescription for a hundred already renewed four times. They gave her some anchorage, but she was puzzled by some of the dreams they evoked and the sudden wakening to a world it took her minutes to apprehend; when she drifted back again into slumber it was usually to a peaceful nothingness that even a bout of Adda's muttering restlessness did not disturb, beyond rousing her briefly. It was in nights of exceptionally vivid dreams that she had become aware of another self inside her, shadowy yet inescapable, an element of vehement hatred streaking through it with lightning force. Once, she had dreamt that Mrs Pyle-Williams, President of the Women's Guild, had turned into a strong, talking eel, one moment reared up on the platform of a meeting, the next slithering on a board, still talking while the fishmonger in Melin chopped it up into convenient pieces.

That night there was a red-horned ram. First, he lay on the steps of the War Memorial in Bedd, then, his flourish of horns down, charged towards her where she stood unable to move, waiting isolated but entirely without alarm. At the moment of impact she woke to a consciousness broken to smithereens, but also intact, the smashed pieces slowly assembling and bringing a strange feeling of relaxation. When, soon, she drifted back into sleep, another dream came, elusive and without the force of the other. Two small, wraith-like figures, blurred children, ran towards her on a long ribbon of bare road, and she knew she was far, far away in Australia.

Police Superintendent Cosker, after a telephone conversation with her, arrived from Melin in his car the following evening. She took him into the living room and offered refreshment, which he declined, as he did a chair; he had an air of not intending to stay long. She placed herself on a chair at the table as if needing support in her ordeal of anxiety. Bulky of frame, a frown natural to his swarthy, broad, hard-muscled face, Cosker loomed near her like a black cloud that might suddenly drench a person with cold rain.

When she began to launch into a recital of the trip to Pen Mawr, he interrupted her. 'Yes, yes, Constable Vaughan has reported in full about that. Do you know whether your husband drew a large sum of money from his bank recently?'

'He hasn't. I looked over his cheque book stubs this morning.' She had forced the bureau open with a chisel soon after a sustaining breakfast; its key was on the ring of them Adda always carried in his trousers pocket.

Approval of her seemed to lighten Cosker's overcast face as he continued, 'Sorry to ask, but had there been any unpleasantness lately?' His tone said, 'From either you or him?'

'Unpleasantness? We've been married for forty years. His temper was short now and again, of course, but we never went into any nasty dispute.'

Had Cosker come just to look at her? He said, 'Well, all I can do just now is send an officer on the walk from Pen Mawr to Dulais. That will be tomorrow. It's deserted up there as a rule.'

With a touch of resentment, she said, 'Shouldn't a man have been sent today? I told Vaughan on the phone this morning that the bus driver said that nobody of Adda's description got on his bus at Dulais or at stops on the way to Bedd. Only four passengers, three women and a young man, all known to him by sight. He thought he remembered Adda from journeys before.'

'There's still time for him to turn up. In any case, no officer was available to take the walk today. Your husband is a healthy man, I understand, and takes good care of himself.'

'Of his body,' she corrected. 'When I met a Melin lady picking blackberries, Mrs Edwards, living in Mabon Road, I remember telling her how he went for these long walks, and at home he skipped with a rope every morning and used dumb-bells as well.'

Cosker patiently listened, and asked, 'No history of nervous breakdown?'

'His temper became shorter the last year or two. Moped now and again since he retired from the Gas Board. Tossed and turned and muttered in his sleep, wakening me sometimes. But it didn't make me worried.'

'We had a case last year in Melin of loss of memory. Man was found in . . . '

'Vaughan told me,' she interrupted in turn. 'A hundred pounds on him.'

'Well, if nothing results tomorrow I will report him missing and it will be circulated. You have a recent photograph of him?'

'There's one of him taken with the Bowling Club members. Adda wasn't a man to go to a photographer, though I told him he ought to send one of him and me to our daughter in Australia, married with two children that haven't seen us yet. We intend going there soon and . . . '

'Give Vaughan the Bowling Club photograph after tomorrow, if necessary. Any relations he could have gone to?'

'Everybody's dead, except Marged, our daughter in Australia that . . . '

'Friends?' Cosker continued, in the bringing-to-heel manner of his profession. Turning his head to face her squarely, he gave her a skimmingly quick look.

She returned this scrutiny with no evidence of evasion, although, before she replied, four or five seconds passed, as was need to take thought. 'Nobody that wouldn't let me know he was with them.'

The superintendent left without further questioning. It seemed plain that he, like P.C. Vaughan, thought that this case could be merely another example of a husband going off either because of temporary amnesia or, more likely, a private dispute which his wife preferred not to disclose.

That night she again took a double dose of sleeping tablets, and, elusive among dreams which were neither pleasant nor alarming, she had a fleeting glimpse of the red-horned ram, his posterior facing her. Waking at four o'clock, she went downstairs and prepared a cup of hot malted milk, reputed to induce untroubled sleep. It applied that night.

Of course, news that Adda was missing became known throughout Bedd before any official declaration of it was made. Vaughan had telephoned her in the evening following the Superintendent's visit and reported that the officer dispatched to cover the walk from Pen Mawr to Dulais found nothing. There was only one track the whole seven miles, but since her husband was familiar with the route it was unlikely he had got lost up there; besides, only a child would get lost or bewildered in such an area. Accident could not be ruled out; here and there the track went perilously close to the edge of the cliffs. Did her husband suffer from attacks of giddiness? Was his heart sound? Rhonwen, her voice pitched high, said he never had cause to consult Dr Llewellyn and he never complained of anything. She promised to search for the Bowling

Club photograph.

Three members of the Women's Guild telephoned the next day to commiserate, their questions carefully pruned of inquisitiveness. One offered to keep her company in the house and even sleep there. Rhonwen, voice pitched low, admitted to anxiety, and said she thought the police suspected loss of memory. No, she'd prefer not to have visitors yet. Then, two days later, the Superintendent himself telephoned, uttered a very few preliminary words intended to prepare her for bad news, and said her husband had been found. She gave a high-pitched cry before he continued. The owner of a motor boat cruising in the bay had detected the body through binoculars. Gulls were swooping over it on the rocks below Pen Mawr. It had already been removed at low tide by lifeboat men from Dulais. Identity was established from a letter in a pocket; it contained a cheque for payment of rates.

Her second cry became a wail. The Superintendent offered sympathy. Controlling herself, Rhonwen asked, 'Where can I see him?'

He paused, then said, 'I am unable to tell you yet. There is no mortuary at Dulais.'

'I want to see him at once!'

Another pause. 'Best not. He will be brought to the Melin mortuary. But best not to see him.'

'Why? Why?'

In a more deliberate way, a man taking a necessarily firm stand with an overwrought woman, he answered, 'For one thing, his eyes are gone'. He added, 'We can overlook the rule for the next of kin to give identification. Constable Vaughan knew him.'

There was a post-mortem, and then the body lay coffined in the funeral parlour of Thomas Tucker & Sons in Melin. The police did not visit her again, but P.C. Vaughan kept her informed by telephone and said there would be an inquest which she must attend. A reporter in the Melin weekly paper telephoned to ask if he might call on her; she refused at once. But she did not evade a visit from the President of the Women's Guild.

For this occasion Mrs Pyle-Williams obliterated her mysterious dislike of Rhonwen — one of those antipathies between two women that can as suddenly submerge as surface. She was an ambassador from talking Bedd, by-passing police deductions and procedures, exercising local judgement of far more influence than laws formulated in England. Rhonwen suggested tea. She wore a black cardigan and a dark purple neck-scarf. A large silver tray lay ready on the table, on it Rhonwen's best cups and saucers, a fluted silver teapot and a home-knitted cosy beside it, scones, a cake and a pot of newly made bramble jelly. Mrs Pyle-Williams' car had given a warning hoot as it entered the front garden of Cartref. In the living room she trotted to a fireside chair, shaking out and adjusting a cushion in her usual decisive way. She wore a suit of strong Welsh tweed and a felt hat with a long pheasant tail feather sticking out from it, firm as a sword.

'I've come with the sympathy of the W.G. members,' she began, in her florid, speech-making manner. 'You were not expected at yesterday's meeting, of course. It was full, every other member there except P.C. Vaughan's wife — one of her twins has measles and the other is expected to be infected. It was decided unanimously that I should telephone and offer to call on you. Your monthly financial report, now due, can be postponed.'

Although she had been in the house many times before, when it was Rhonwen's turn in the rota committee meetings of six members, her gaze roved about the spick-and-span room and settled approvingly on the gleamingly ceremonious teapot, given a polish immediately after her telephone call. An active woman, she dealt in house property when opportunity came her way, buying a ramshackle cottage or barn and renovating it for sale, though, as a Nationalist, it was her practice not to accept an English buyer even if this was to her financial advantage. Steadfast guardian of the district's monuments and lore, it was while she was on a long visit to relations in North Wales that the English-born academic at Aberystwyth stole a march on her by snapping up his holiday cottage at a bargain price; that later he cast doubt on the myth of the druid priestess turned to stone added insult to injury.

Rhonwen went to the kitchen to fill the teapot and, returned, said in her quiet way, 'They think the inquest will be on Monday.' Her air of stoical endurance did not change. She was very much a daughter of an old, old race.

'I've heard they've already had a post-mortem.'

'They wouldn't let me see him.'

'*Wouldn't?*' Characteristic militancy sounded. 'You could insist. I will go with you if you like.'

'Well,' Rhonwen corrected herself, 'Police Superintendent Cosker advised me not to see him. The seagulls had been at his face.' She had sat at the table before the laden tray.

'Shall I come to the table?'

'You'll be more comfortable there just for tea.' It was a way of indicating that the visit was not expected to be of long duration. Rhonwen placed a low table before the visitor, brought a cup of tea, paper napkin, buttered scone and pot of bramble jelly. 'The jelly hasn't set properly yet. Made the day after Adda left me, from blackberries I picked with a Melin lady I met just after dropping Adda on the way to Pen Mawr. Making the jelly kept my mind occupied. Six pounds and eight ounces of berries, weighed on my brass scales that I bought from Matthews, weights included, when he closed his old-established shop and retired to Tenby.' A cloudiness gained on her while Mrs Pyle-Williams opened the scone and took two spoonfuls of jelly. 'It's all been too big for me, so far, the shock. I shall be trying not to go under, and take things one by one, as they come.'

Mrs Pyle-Williams looked at her with even more approval than was given to the heirloom teapot. She approved what sounded like a hint that dwelling unduly on the tragedy was not expected or wished. 'The jelly tastes beautiful,' she complimented, 'runny, but fresh, fresh.'

Rhonwen sat gazing at the window and its view of clean-outlined mountains. 'It was an accident. He must have slipped while doing his exercises, though he didn't take his skipping-rope that day. There was no reason at all for him to kill himself. We were going to see Marged in Australia next year.'

'Don't grieve, my girl, don't grieve.' The president's voice had found the proper key, pianissimo, though with a hearty undercurrent. 'Too soon to talk, but if it was me I would move to another house. It makes one *do* things gain, sets the blood pumping in a new way.' As a woman who had been married and widowed twice, she might have meant too that Rhonwen was still of an age when another husband would be in order.

'There'll be a lot of things for the October jumble sale,' Rhonwen said, emerging slightly from her abstraction. 'All his clothes.'

'It'll be on the 24th of October, *not* the 25th. The vicar's wife told us the Memorial Hall was booked for a Flannel Dance on the 24th. A muddle.' With a second cup of tea, the president welcomed another scone and a slice of cake, getting up considerately to fetch these.

Rhonwen, who had eaten nothing, poured herself a second cup. 'I sent a letter air-mail to Marged,' she said, fidgeting with a knife.

'You didn't cable her?'

'A cable might upset her, I thought, and I couldn't say everything in it.'

'You wouldn't go and live with her in New Zealand?' If so, there would be a house for sale and Cartref was beautifully situated.

'Australia it is.' The cloudiness remained, vaguely entranced. 'I must wait.'

'Oh, don't *brood*, my girl. Say to yourself soon as you waken "I'll fill the day chock-full". Look, will you take full charge of the jumble sale? Mrs Pryce-Morris won't mind giving it up to you. There's your car to go round the farms and houses collecting. The typed circulars are going out soon, and an advert in the Melin paper.'

'Adda and I were going to go to Torquay for a week in October.'

The president banged her fist, not too violently, on the wide arm of her chair. 'You mustn't brood, *cariad*.'

'I *want* to brood.' Rhonwen half-whimpered now. 'It *was* an accident. Adda wouldn't want to destroy himself.' She suddenly demanded, 'Are they saying that in Bedd?'

'Who's saying what? Nobody is saying anything that I've heard.'

'He booked a week at The Torquay hotel himself . . . . A boarding house,' Rhonwen corrected herself, 'because we were saving up for going on the sea cruise next year. I must write and cancel the booking.'

'They might ask for a percentage of the board and lodge charge, so mind to tell them it's because of your husband's unexpected death. People can show heart sometimes.'

'We used to go to a tip-top hotel; our room in the front with a view over the bay . . . . Then he began to save money on this and that, and I thought "Is he putting it on horses or something?".' Rhonwen added, 'He couldn't cope with retirement.'

'Mind *you* do! Staying moping at home will bring you down. Women can go cranky with it. Shall I put your name as collector for the jumble sale?' Normally the name of Mrs Pryce-Morris would have carried more weight as a collector of items, sometimes of worth, but there was much to be said for that of a tragic widow. Proceeds of the sale, together with two stalls of home-made products such as cakes, chutney, jams, and with luck, hand-stitched bed quilts, went towards obliging very poor and old women to take a coach trip in the Spring to such places as Llandrindod Wells or Builth. It was Rhonwen's province to take charge of all the accounts and moneys.

She declined the collection task and gave no indication that the well-meaning visitor was lacking in tact. Even in these changed times a newly bereaved widow should remain in mourning seclusion for a while. However, when Mrs Pyle-Williams, who knew everybody of consequence, rose to go she gave a hint of active moral support.

'I expect the inquest coroner will be Vavasour Johns,' she said. 'I am friendly with his wife, Babs, and I will be seeing her on market day in Melin tomorrow, for coffee in the Tudor café.' Did she mean that she would be supplying a character testimonial regarding the W.G. treasurer, or that any ordeal Rhonwen might have to endure at the inquest would be eased, perhaps to the extent of not being called to give evidence and have her domestic life gone into? Rhonwen accompanied her to her car. Admiring the front garden's condition, Mrs Pryce-Williams murmured, 'If you want to live with your daughter in New Zealand you would get a good price for this property.'

'Australia is where Marged lives.'

'They're next door to each other. Plenty of Welsh people in both places, no doubt, so no need to feel homesick. They're not Japan or India. Christian like us.' A semi-professional eye ran over the frontage of the thick-walled old house, plain, square, flat-windowed, endurance in its severity. 'One of the best houses in Bedd for views. Bleak, though, and a bad lane up to it. All the same, I would like to be offered first refusal if you decide to sell.'

'Adda was planning to have it whitewashed before we went to Australia to see Marged.'

'Needs it. Bad flaking. Exposed to all the winter storms up here. That might knock two or three hundred pounds off a valuation. Go to Lloyd's in Melin if you have the house whitewashed. They did new chimney cowls and a few slates for me eight pounds cheaper than Rowlands' estimate.' Rhonwen's shoulder was patted and the pheasant feather tickled her face as Bedd's militant protector leaned out of her car window. 'The W.G. will be arranging to send a wreath and four or five members will attend the funeral, besides myself. Now don't worry about the inquest.' Village bickerings, criticism and malice were in order when a healthy and respectable person could retaliate, but ranks closed loyally when real disaster struck.

Probably due to Mrs Pyle-Williams' influence, Rhonwen was not called to the witness stand in the Melin Town Hall room. The coroner, plump-chested Vavasour Johns, had the air of a sleepy pigeon, and his after-lunch inquest could have been assessed and clarified beforehand. It was remarkably short. The only persons called to speak were P.C. Vaughan and the Melin hospital surgeon who had conducted the post-mortem and said injuries of the deceased included a fractured skull and death was instantaneous. More lengthy, P.C. Vaughan, consulting his notebook frequently, related being called by the wife of the deceased and the information she had given him, including her husband getting out of their car near Pen Mawr while she gathered blackberries, meeting by chance Mrs Judith Edwards, residing at 27 Mabon Road, Melin. The deceased was in the habit of walking to Dulais and also did physical exercises at the pinnacle of Pen Mawr, including use of a skipping rope. He was apparently in good health and had never consulted the family doctor. His wife had said that there was nothing unusual in his manner that day. They had plans to visit their daughter in Australia next year. Pen Mawr pinnacle had been examined and a subsidence of the grassy verge between gorse bushes was discovered; it could easily have escaped notice, clumps of vegetation still protruding from slippery clay and crumbling chalk.

There was no jury; evidently the coroner had decided this was not a case for the calling of such. Johns, after a few preliminary words referring to no evidence of suspicious circumstances, brought in a verdict of accidental death and followed it with a valedictory appreciation of the deceased, greatly respected in a long career with the Gas Board. The appreciation was really directed at the widow, sitting flanked by Mrs Pyle-Williams and three less important members of the Bedd Women's Guild. An audibly breathing reporter from the local weekly was present too. Later, Rhonwen learnt that Mrs Edwards of Mabon Road had been visited by P.C. Vaughan and told she might be required to attend the inquest; since she was not there, it seemed more evident that the whole business had been sifted out earlier.

Outside the Town Hall, Rhonwen said that no, she did not wish anyone to go home with her. Her car was parked round the corner, and she moved towards it with the blank endurance in her face unchanged by relief that the ordeal was over, though a small petal of red in her cheeks could have come from tension. Mrs Pyle-Williams escorted her to the car. 'You have heard from your daughter?' she asked.

'Marged? No. Letters by air take four or five days from Australia.'

'I expect she will want you to go out to her now,' the escort comforted. 'Plenty of people of all ages settle down happily in those places . . . . *Cariad*, take a nap soon as you reach home.'

'Insurance Evans is coming to see me at six. I think he's been waiting for the inquest verdict.'

From the wheel, Rhonwen did not forget to thank the W.G. president for her help and support; this veiled reference to possible interference on her behalf was dismissed by a nod and a wave of the hand. Mrs Pyle-Williams always aided in any way that would keep her beloved countryside and its true natives immaculate, as far as was possible. It was she who had instigated a successful move to prevent the construction of an extensive reservoir in the Vale of Bedd Einion, with its sacred sepulchre and other myths out of the skull of history.

Insurance Evans arrived promptly. He had learnt of the inquest verdict in the Einion Arms, which opens for the evening licensed hours at five, though of course a hard-pressed Bedd man could always go through the old coaching yard at the side and buy a drink in Ben Bowen's back room at any time. P.C. Vaughan, returning fast on his bike, told him of the verdict.

'It means the matter is simple now,' he said to Rhonwen, accepting a generous amount of brandy from a seldom-used bottle. He wore a black tie and settled in the deep lounge chair, his solid width as reassuring as the policies sensible people entrusted to his care.

Rhonwen somewhat eased an initial hesitancy in his deferential but cautious manner; she knew the conditions of the insurance policy on Adda's life, and replied, 'Yes. But even if it had been suicide there'd be no difference, would there? Adda took the policy out twenty years ago, not two. A man or woman must commit suicide in two years for the beneficiary to lose the lump sum due. How long before the money comes?'

This new widow was not wasting time in useless grieving. Neither was there a lack of business drive. Only a touch of surprise lay in Evans's question — 'You want the money at once?'

'No. There's no heavy debts to pay. But I am wanting to make my plans.'

'I can tell my Company the matter is urgent,' he promised, kindling to her a little more. 'The cheque for two thousand pounds could be arriving in a fortnight, or less.'

'I like things clear. You know I am treasurer of the Women's Guild. Everything exact to the last penny in my books. Adda taught me how to keep accounts and draw up a balance sheet.' She might have been talking of her pair of shop brass scales in the kitchen, with its row of weights ranging from two pounds to half an ounce.

Evans took courage from the fact that she had asked him to call immediately after the inquest, a request which at first had struck him as precipitate. 'Adda,' he offered, his eye lurking on and off her with admiring, yet still half-uncertain respect, 'will be leaving a sad blank in the Bowling Club.' A light suddenly came into his widower's gaze as she continued to sit quite still at the table, her hands clasped on the well-polished wood, a lonely widow's hands. 'Rhonwen,' he plunged, 'you want someone to take charge of the funeral arrangements? A man friend?'

She answered at once, 'Yes.'

'I knew Adda all his life. You would like me to take charge?' At her nod, he paid her the tribute of a celerity equal to her own. 'Thomas Tucker & Sons in Melin will be best. Old-established. Those new people in Dinas Road, calling themselves Funeral Furnishers as if they're ashamed of "Undertakers" — well, they've got swank cars, and I daresay they have to be paid for at a swank price.'

'The arrangements so far are made with Tucker's. Adda's body is in their parlour.'

'Cremation is it to be? There are wishes in Adda's will?'

'No. His will and mine are at Madoc Howells, Solicitor in Melin. We went there together after Marged had gone to Australia many years ago. Burial or cremation was left for me or him to decide, for whoever went first. I want him cremated.'

'Modern. Modern.' Evans spoke in a suitably reduced tone, but admiration was accumulating. 'Leave it all to me. I will be representing the Bowling Club,' — he meant in affectionate labours, a melancholy burden for the lone widow, her only blood relation in Australia — 'and some of the other members will turn up at the crematorium, no doubt. Flowers?'

'Yes.'

He took out a pocket diary, drew a pencil from its spine, and finished the brandy on the low table beside him. 'Memorial cards? There's a printer in Melin and I have seen the tasteful wedding invitations he draws up.' He suggested fifty cards. She told him membership of the Women's Guild alone amounted to sixty-five, and he said, 'Then a hundred. Won't be much dearer than fifty. It's the setting up that costs . . . . Now Rhonwen,' he proceeded, 'what is the date you think best? The undertaker will have to arrange with the crematorium and it must fit in. Last January, when they were so busy, Lily Locke had to be kept eleven days, so full up they were mornings and afternoons.'

'The solicitor can handle all this?' she asked, emerging from a lapse into musing.

'That's for you to choose. Shall I go to see him early tomorrow and say I am taking charge? Save his cost, Rhonwen.'

Agreeing to this, she rose to pour him more brandy.

'I will open a subscription for a wreath from the Bowling Club tomorrow,' he said. 'A sheet pinned on our green baize board, with my name first.' He took a sip of brandy. 'Adda and you . . . valued old clients of mine.' Her own life was insured for a similar amount of two thousand pounds, and the premiums were never paid late to the collector, unlike some clients in Bedd and district.

Other items were decided, such as insertion of an announcement in the Melin paper after the cremation date was settled the next day. Evans made no move to leave for home, where, his three children long out in the world — one teaching in the Rhondda, one married to a Cardiff publican and one a chapel minister in Llanelli — he had lived alone since his wife's death, a Bedd woman going in most days to keep his house clean and tidy. Perhaps Rhonwen would ask him to stay for a meal. That she did not display embarrassing grief made him hopeful. The old carriage clock on the sideboard ticked away delicately. His diary closed, he spoke in sincere admiration of Adda, recalling several little episodes at the Bowling Club, including Adda's triumphant performance in a contest with a visiting team. 'Took care of his body,' he said; 'proud of it.'

'Why did he hit Emlyn Price on the head?' she interrupted this flow. 'Adda wasn't much of a drinker at all. He told me the quarrel was only a bit of an argument about politics, but I didn't believe him.'

Evans paused for a moment, decided she could receive specific information, and said, 'Emlyn called him a randy old goat. Emlyn's tongue gets loose in drink.'

'Adda wasn't a randy old goat,' she commented, not an eyelid flickering. 'A wife always knows, unless she's a fool or wants to be.' She went on at a tangent, 'I remember he wanted to keep a couple of goats in our back garden, but I wouldn't have it. He thought goat's milk was good for his body.'

'Emlyn's mouth is as big as Twm Shon Catti's cave. Men talk a lot of rude nonsense when they are together, you see, Rhonwen,' Evans reassured her. 'No one takes notice as a rule. Adda must have been feeling out of sorts that evening in the pavilion.'

'I am praying I won't miss him too much,' she murmured.

For the first time in his visit she looked at her visitor in a full, and pensive, way, as he sat there filling the spacious chair with his safe bulk, a man successful in his work, as unblemished in repute as she was, near her own age, and not nearly ready for retirement. He was the kind of man a lonely woman would go to for advice of most kinds. His insurance work overflowed into his whole character. Fat was not supposed to be healthy, but his seemed to breed a security beyond the policies issued by a long-established London company that was not likely to let one down. She had always approved him, and as a physical specimen he was a contrast to sinewy, figure-obsessed Adda, a relaxing contrast and a change.

'Well,' he said, stroking his substantial neck, 'I shall do all the errands tomorrow, by phone and in person. The solicitor must apply for the state grant towards funeral costs. Probate was granted quickly for my Gwen's estate, such as it was.' He brought in his wife's name as if it was a reminder to himself. Theirs had been a happy marriage, and therefore he was predisposed to appreciation of the condition in general. Nevertheless, as if on an abrupt decision, he soon rose to go. He clasped her hand in both his own, holding it for almost a minute, an excusable gesture on such an evening, the inquest worry gone. Yet still some element in her made him tentative and uncertain. His urge was willing, but its generating spark remained weak.

That night the red-horned ram came back. On this occasion he appeared in the hinterland between sleep and waking, when uncaught remnants of another dimension persist and are slowly dispersed by emerging reality — a bed, faint grey light at a window, and need to make water. The ram seemed to be galloping along a frieze of bushes, and there was a sense of hooves pounding on hard ground; he stopped, turned to look at her, and below the terrible horns his eyes shone red as them. Head down, he was going to charge her, and she would be smashed to smithereens again. Her eyes were closed, but wasn't she awake, a long dream faded away and the ram gone? She opened her eyes and saw the misty outline of the window.

She went downstairs, made tea, and, drinking, the silence of the house was reassuring. Absence of another person brought a different quality to it, no expectancy of discord lurking. For a while, deciding not to return to bed, she played with the pair of brass scales and weights on the kitchen table, as she often did on house-bound winter days, weighing out into paper bags measures of sugar, tea, breakfast oats and stores of other goods kept in light large black-and-gold tin canisters, also acquired from the closing-down old tradesman in the village. It had been one of her girlhood dreams to open and rule a shop, and had she not become so fully in love with Adda it was what she would have done. She mused on a similar speculation now, while light increased at the window. Would she be able to open a shop in Australia? There would be capital enough for a modest venture.

When Insurance Evans visited her the next evening, and had concluded a report on his achievements for her that day, she asked, 'Are there red-horned rams hereabouts?'.

He looked up from the notes in his diary. 'I never saw any. Always black horns.'

'I thought I saw one on the day I lost Adda.' All the explanation she gave of her pointless question was, 'I had finished picking blackberries and was following the car of Mrs Edwards, a Melin lady, and behind a gate I thought I saw a red-horned ram staring at me nastily.' She sat at the table as before, hands clasped, eyes directed at the window.

Evans shifted his behind slightly, and also the spectacles he wore for reading and accountancy. Was she suffering from the effect of delayed shock? 'Come now, Rhonwen, you're not thinking it was an omen, are you? It was only a sheep, red horns or not. Thousands of sheep hereabouts. I am sick of the sight and sound of them on my rounds, collecting my premiums from the farmhouses. All alike. Sheep don't have character.'

'Oh, yes, they do. There's savagery in them when they're together. They've got a language.'

'Only a shaky *mare, mare, mare*, surely? I daresay a ewe can be touchy when her lambs haven't grown to full strength and a stranger walks near. But savage, no.'

'A ram, I meant.'

He took a sip of brandy. The labelled bottle on the sideboard was nearing its end, and he meant to remind her that, in view of possible callers with condolences and a gathering after the cremation, he should order for her at the Einion Arms a supply of assorted drinks. 'No doubt a ram could be nasty, according to circumstances, but I would cross a field with a dozen of them in it. With cattle and stock you mustn't feel or show fright. They smell it and get upset themselves.'

'I never saw a red-horned ram before,' she said, still gazing fixedly through the window.

To lighten her melancholy, he related an anecdote. 'It's true that even a ewe can be bad-tempered when provoked. You heard about the lamb that Miss Mari Hopcyns stole?' Her attention drawn, Rhonwen shook her head. 'Lives in those rows of houses called Rhobell Street. Well, you know some sheep come down at night from the low hillsides and roam through the back lanes of streets for food in the rubbish buckets collected early on Monday and Friday mornings. One Sunday night last spring Mari went to place a second bucket outside her back garden door and there she found a ewe and a young lamb eating cabbage leaves out of the other bucket. She snatched up the pretty little lamb and slammed the door. Four days she had it in her house, living alone, an old maid with peculiar ways, seldom going out, and wouldn't insure her house or her life. Then on the Thursday night she went to place a bucket as usual, ready for collection next morning, and there was the ewe waiting for her. Soon as she opened the door it butted her, and Mari went sprawling and the bucket flying. The ewe flashed down the garden path crying "*mare, mare,*" and skedaddled into the house. The lamb, Mari's neighbours say, was lying on the fireside rug with a titty bottle of milk beside it. '*Mare, mare,*' the mother bleated louder, and in a second both of them were out of the house, jumping over Mari lying panting on the path . . . . Ha! ha!' He peeped across at Rhonwen, uncertain whether the anecdote was welcome at such a time.

'They've got senses we don't possess,' she murmured, still preoccupied.

'How could a sheep know the days of the week, though? Know

Mari's buckets were put out on Sunday and Thursday nights?'

'Second sight.'

'I heard about Mari in the Bowling Club. Dr Llewellyn had to attend her for bruises and nerves. Shock. We must be careful of shock, Rhonwen. Not allow it to take hold.' He eased his frontage. 'Say to ourselves, "Life must go on the same". You must attend the W.G. meetings soon again. Mrs Pyle-Williams told me she's persuaded our M.P. to give a talk during the next Parliament recess.'

'Before that,' the treasurer said, recalled to precision, 'we've got Sir John Watcyns talking about Egypt and showing toy films he took of tombs and statues. Hire of the projector and screen is going to cost ten pounds. Is it worth the money? I voted against it but Mrs Pyle-Williams wants to let Sir John show off.'

'His talk in English or Welsh?' Evans was glad of her side-tracking into normal events. A vague unease had kept returning to him.

'English. Only about half of the members can follow Welsh properly. Mrs Pyle-Williams wanted to start Welsh lessons for the others, but they voted against it. One of them said, "We come here to enjoy ourselves. Our blackboard and chalk days are over".'

'A pity.' Evans was bilingual, as was necessary on his professional rounds, calling at remote farmhouses which had been there for centuries, many of the elderly in them unable to speak English.

'Now,' he reverted to the reasons for his present visit, and about to terminate it, 'I have put the matter of Adda's life insurance in hand today, soon as I knew officially from the Town Hall that his death certificate was made out. I told my company payment should be made without delay. They need a poke about payments sometimes. Why should you lose a few weeks' interest on two thousand pounds?'

A token of thanks for his industry was due. She said, 'You must have something of Adda's to remember him by. There's a gold watch he was wearing when he fell down the cliff. The police have given it to me, and a bunch of his keys.' Her eyes strayed to his bureau in a corner of the room. 'His pocket watch was soaked by the tide washing over the rocks. But the watch is going again. Waterproof, and pure gold. He chose it for his retirement gift from the Gas Board.'

'Later on, Rhonwen, thank you very much, later on.' He glanced at his own steel-cased watch. 'Now I am calling at the Einion Arms on my way home — it is the day when the bus leaves a box of fish there for Ben Bowen's wife to sell, if you remember, and I am buying a hake. You would like me to order drinks to be delivered here by Ben?'

'I don't want mourners to come back here after the funeral. One at a time is all I can welcome.'

'Quite right,' he agreed promptly. 'The circumstances for you are different than is usual. All the same . . . '

'Two bottles of sherry, two of whisky, two of brandy, two of gin,' she decided nevertheless, 'one of the sherry sweet, the other dry.'

He jotted the order into his diary. Her grasp of matters was satisfactory; as yet, there was only that one sign of delayed shock, imagining a red-horned ram was interested in her. He lingered a few minutes more, indecision in his departure as before. She continued to sit at the bare table. In the evening light she looked younger, the clear oval of her face almost that of a woman under forty because of her soft-tinted complexion and the true blue of her eyes and no threads of grey in her dark hair. She had kept her slender figure too. His eyes paused on her, strayed, returned, strayed.

'Mrs Bowen will sell all the hake if I don't hurry,' he said, harassed. 'Fish fresh from the sea today!'

Rhonwen paused before suggesting, her tone not really encouraging, 'You can phone her.'

'I told Dafydd Griffiths I would be there at seven. Wants to see me about a hayloft that went on fire. So I'd best be off now.' He rose and gave her shoulder a pat. 'See myself out . . . .'

She remained at the table, and he did not hear her murmur, 'Ask him about red-horned rams.' She herself couldn't recall noticing such on the few occasions when she visited Melin's stinking cattle and stock market on Tuesdays. Her thoughts strayed to goats. For what reason had that Bowling Club member called Adda a randy old goat? How much was known of him among that private brood of men?

The inquest was given a short report in the Melin weekly paper. Its only personal items stated that the deceased was a founder member of the Bedd Einion Bowling Club and left a widow and a married daughter who had emigrated to Australia. Had Mrs Pyle-Williams brought more curbing influence to bear?

Insurance Evans did not pay another visit to Cartref before the funeral. He told Rhonwen on the telephone that he had ordered three cars for the mourners selected by her to receive special invitations, who would assemble at the undertakers where Adda's body lay in a closed coffin, also chosen and described by her considerate helpmate. She expected no mourners to assemble at the house and accompany her and did not want a funeral car to collect her, since she had her own car to take her to the undertakers, maroon in colour though it was. 'Modern, modern,' he assented again. 'The old days are gone.' He meant that in those days the coffin would be in the occupant's home, a crowd gathering there for a brief service, and a Welsh hymn sung as it was borne out to a crystal-paned hearse, every front window of the house shrouded, and the melodious lamentation heard down and up much of the vale.

Rhonwen responded to the old days to the extent of wearing unrelieved black, obtained in a new, ambitious Melin shop that went so far as to call itself a Boutique. Mrs Pyle-Williams and Insurance Evans sat with her in the first car; the other two carried members of the W.G., including P.C. Vaughan's wife, a head clerk from the Gas Board and three members of the Bowling Club. The flower-decked hearse had gone ahead, at a more rapid pace than the mourners' cars.

The three miles' journey to the crematorium, a brick structure built a few years earlier on an extension of the old Melin cemetery, took fifteen minutes, and the tailored service in the chapel exactly the same time. The handsome coffin, with Rhonwen's wreath alone on it, slid out of view and a pair of cupboard-like doors closed behind it with the same foreboding invisibility of manipulation by live human hands as they had opened. Outside the chapel the mourners assembled to press Rhonwen's hand, murmur a few words, then chat among themselves and examine the floral tributes spread on a paved terrace. Insurance Evans continued to take charge of Rhonwen, which, discreet as it was, did not escape notice. Mrs Pyle-Williams held an animated discussion with a close group and did not inspect the flowers. Rhonwen detached herself from everyone and stepped across to the display, bending to read each card on the wreaths and sprays. Her need to be alone for this was respected by all, including Evans.

There were about a dozen tributes, not one of them exceptional or ornate enough to make anyone stop for more than a moment, to read the attached card. Rhonwen paused longest over a card fastened to a spray of white and yellow chrysanthemums set on a bed of evergreens. Yet the only name on the card, printed in a corner, was that of a Melin florist shop. Odder still, an inscription on the card was typewritten. It ran: *From a friend, with deepest sympathy.*

Two days later an air-mail letter arrived from Marged.

*Dear Mam,*

*Well, Joseph and I were surprised to receive your letter telling us about Dad. You must be upset and I am writing at once to say Joseph and I are thinking about you. I hope you will write again soon and say how and why it all happened. Found dead below Pen Mawr is not saying much.*

*You will be sorry to hear that a fortnight ago Joseph was home ill with a very bad stomach and did not go to the bank for a week. But Linda May and Joseph Small are both well as I am. Linda May asked what a grandfather was, she is quite backward in some things, but eats like a horse and is getting quite fat. Joseph Small, well, I am worried about him not eating enough but he is interested in everything and not dull in his talk. He is six on December 15, and Linda May eight on December 18. I often wonder why they are so near in birthdays, meaning two parties for their friends, then Christmas ones coming so soon after. I know you will not forget their birthdays, but if it's little parcels, send by air, as by sea is not reliable for dates. Money is best really. Linda May said last week, what is Wales, where is it, can I go there on a bike? She is silly quite often, surprising me, but her father says she will expand later, meaning in her mind. He says she takes after me and Joseph Small after him. I blame his stomach when he is aggravating, which is more often now. The three keep me busy and I am glad Joseph has gone back to work again. I sleep like a log, worn out, which is not surprising. I forget if I told you this new house has eight rooms, and you know how mad I am against dust. No more this time. Joseph has just come home from the bank.*

*Your loving daughter, Marged.*

*P.S. Joseph says, ask your mother if he made a will. He is surprised you didn't mention it.*

Eight rooms, and not one offered to her mother! Not even a word about the planned trip to Australia, mentioned in letters from Cartref over the past two years. But wasn't there time yet for an invitation to settle in Australia? Re-reading the letter, Rhonwen felt in her bones that no invitation would come. There was to be no escape to that new world where a child could ask 'What is Wales, where is it?'. Marged had always been complete in her own skin, like her father. Wasn't it to be expected that the two children, born of herself, absorbed her to the exclusion of anyone else, perhaps including her husband now? Rhonwen read the letter yet again and told herself it was perfectly natural that Joseph should enquire about a will.

Should Marged be told that, in her parents' wills, she would be the sole inheritor when the survivor died? No, let quiet about the matter remain as it was. Information about wills was best kept secret. Nevertheless, her mother had no intention of altering the existing will. Marged was still Adda's and her sacred contribution to their line and heritage. Across all those vast waters the ancient line continued in Linda May and Joseph Small. Even if ever her mother decided to marry again she would not tell a prospective husband of the will. Let him bring his own substance. She would not marry a poor man.

Of course, she could spend a lot of money on herself before she died. On what? Fur coats, a splendid new car, best quality tours to those famous European places the advertisements for which she had read without ever relating them to herself. Marged's letter on the table before her, she sat on in the lucid morning light. Bitter disappointment dwindled further. An old endurance and self-discipline, bred of generations of suppression and strict religious upbringing rose to her aid, and reigned for the moment, the other, darkly mysterious powers gone into abeyance. Let Marged live her own forgetting life across those waters. Also, there was another matter to be dealt with in the near future, an account to settle within easy distance, before the future could be thought of.

Insurance Evans dropped in a week or so after the cremation, bringing a cheque for two thousand pounds. When he put it in her hand, she said, 'Oh, I thought it would come by post,' and tossed it unexamined onto the table.

'It can be done either way, but my company in London think I deal with jungle people down here and they often send me a cheque for delivery in person because some of my clients can't speak or read English, and some can't write either and the settlement document is signed with a cross and witnessed by me and another person. Here is the one for delivery of your little nest-egg, Rhonwen.' Evans offered his important gold-banded fountain pen from among the coloured row of ballpens in his breast pocket. She sighed, and Adda was banished in this other sense without a flicker of recognition that the occasion carried solemnity.

A word of praise for his expeditious zeal on her behalf did not come. The document replaced in its envelope, he sat back in his chair and accepted a whisky from one of the bottles he had ordered for her at the Einion Arms, all standing on the sideboard, one or two opened and half-consumed. 'Anybody been to see you, Rhonwen *fach*?' he asked, allowing himself the commonplace term of endearment with some confidence.

'No, I told Mrs Pyle-Williams on the phone that I wanted to be left alone.' Peculiarly, she added, 'From women, I meant. The W.G. accounts for the month were done and I sent them down to her by Luther the Milk.'

'You are not going to resign from the Guild?' he asked. 'I warned you about letting shock take hold of you.'

She made a gesture with her narrow, somewhat bony hand. It seemed to betray impatience, and her chin jutted out, making her face look less perfectly oval. Then she turned to give him the smile of a woman acknowledging his concern for her. He stirred a little in the chair, not uneasily, but still with an awareness not certain of itself. 'Is there anything of Adda's you would like?' she asked, and then remembered — 'Oh yes; I offered you his gold watch. You would like it or not?'

'Thank you very much. But don't get it now. Another time will do, when you are settled down.' It could have been a hint that this was not expected to be his last visit, social or on business.

She sat back from the table, hands on lap. 'I have been going though his things . . . . Papers first.' She nodded towards his open bureau in a corner of the room; stacks of large, packed envelopes and tied bundles of letters. 'Adda', she said pensively, 'always kept his papers locked up there and carried the key about with him. He used to say "You mustn't muddle your W.G. papers with mine", and I kept them separate in my desk in the other front room.'

Evans' nostrils quivered with interest, and only his shifting gaze hinted at whatever made him appear to be slightly nervous. 'Rhonwen, *fach*, if I can help you with business papers you don't understand, you will ask me?'

'I understand them . . . He kept all his bank statements and stubs of old cheque books, going back for many years. I expect it was the Gas Board training in him.' Her eyes showed a glint, steely and wintry, and unexpected in their mild blue.

'You have heard from your daughter?'

'Yes. I am not going to Australia.'

'A long cruise for a woman to take alone.'

'I meant that I am not going to settle with Marged out there.'

He had not known she had contemplated it. At her invitation, he poured himself another Scotch and water. Really he wanted to know the contents of Adda's will. He imagined the estate to amount to between forty and fifty thousand pounds gross. Making conversation, he told her that so far he had not remembered to inquire if there were red-horned rams in the district.

Her chin jutted out again. She stared at the window as if such a beast would appear there. 'I must have dreamt it. Don't bother to find out.' She went on to speak of sorting Adda's clothes. She wanted them out of the house soon.

Evans lingered. His gaze rested on her with wonder now. She had the demeanour of a woman in whom puritanism and its arid twin, loneliness, would remain in rigid control of her. Would she ever give vent to howling? Sight of even a token dropping of tears would have been welcome to him and perhaps brought out from its decaying hole the old-type male urge to protect and comfort, prior to taking the path to socially legal bedlock. When the tumults and tantrums of the flesh are reduced, money takes a rightful importance in the remaining passions. But still, still, there was that mysterious hampering in him, a hurdle he couldn't understand.

There was something imprisoned in the air about her — a deadlock. The dusk in the room had not yet thickened to the need for electric light, when Evans, with a movement abrupt for him, if only because of his fat, rose from the relaxing chair. 'Dear me, I am due at the Bowling Club to see Moses Treharne about raising funds for buying a new lawn-roller. So excuse me now.' He did not pat her shoulder comfortingly, as he had before. It was as if, running up from all his innards, from his heart and blood, a decision had arrived in his head. The weak spark had sunk lower. She was not for him.

Neither was he for her. But the tribute and attentions of a long courtship would have been a security for her, and by the time she had finally rejected him there surely would have been nothing to haunt her; a business vigour in him would drive away ghosts. As she heard the sharp revving-up of his spluttering old car she knew of his decision. But there would be future business contacts. She reminded herself to send him the gold watch by Luther the Milk, with a formal note of thanks.

She completed many clearance jobs. After the inquest, Mrs Edwards of Mabon Road in Melin had telephoned her from a booth and related that a policeman had called on her to check that she had gathered blackberries with the wife of a missing Bedd man on the applicable afternoon. Rhonwen, feeling no chill, accepted this report of investigation as a proper and lawful duty, showing that the county police were thorough, despite their reputation to the contrary. Mrs Edwards then brought up the matter of the old kitchen dresser and the promise that it could be viewed for possible purchase; she hoped that when all Rhonwen's worries were eased, she and her husband could visit Cartref. Rhonwen apologised for the fussy call of a policeman, and she evaded Mrs Edwards' visit by saying that if later she decided to go and live in Australia the dresser would be offered at a very reasonable price.

She delivered by car to the receiving centre for the W.G. jumble sale Adda's clothes, also his dumb-bells and skipping-rope with the painted wood handles. In addition, she took for the stall of home-made jam, pickles and cakes her stock of bramble jelly. She informed Mrs Pyle-Williams by telephone that she could not attend as stallkeeper at an event that was always so crowded — the strain would be too much, people clustering to stare and sympathise with her. The president, in her downright way, remarked this might be good for sales, and Rhonwen replied with asperity, 'Then put my name on the labels of the pots of bramble jelly and charge a high price for them.'

She went to see Madoc Howells, her solicitor in Melin. He accepted without question her own valuation of the house, which was low; he judged that her net inheritance might amount to over forty thousand pounds, including the life insurance sum. Probate, he thought, should be granted in about a month. The interview was cut-and-dried. Howells' long, bleak face, parsimonious as his talk, conveyed no sympathy for her tragic loss. She left his office in Selyf Place feeling trust in him, liking especially the thin waspish dart of his voice. In the Magistrates' Court at the Town Hall he was well known for successful defence of petty offenders, such as shoplifters and those living at inner fastnesses among the unstained mountains; sometimes, in defence of a bewildered culprit, he would insist on speaking Welsh in court and, should one or more magistrate not understand the native tongue, laboriously and with contempt translate his observations into English. Like Mrs Pyle-Williams, who bore a grudge for never being appointed to sit on the Bench, he was an obdurate Nationalist, though he did not boil to overflowing like her, emotion taking second place to recognition of modern facts such as the growing strength of English barbarians with their purchase of cheap Welsh land for factories.

Her appointment had been in the morning, and after a filling lunch in Melin's leading residential hotel, she fulfilled not the least important of her tasks. Blodwen's, as it is called, is the only florist shop in Melin. Bunches of garden flowers can be bought cheap at market-day stalls, but for ceremonial, social, hospital, wedding and funeral occasions, Blodwen's is where people go. The Christian name of its proprietress was Blodwen, reputed to mean white flower, and she always placed centrally in her crowded window a large vase of white blooms. A professional soprano of short-lived Welsh fame, she forsook artistic hazards for trade and now could not be wheedled from her flowers, indoor plants and cacti, even for charitable events or the annual Horeb festival. Her easy-going sensibility was well known and her shop well stocked. She had taken training with a Bristol male florist. Her funeral wreaths never carried a stale flower.

There was no customer when Rhonwen entered a few minutes after her meal. Blodwen sat in a nook at the back of the shop, eating a wing of chicken off a wad of tissue paper on a table covered with sprays of evergreen, reels of coloured string, large and small scissors, a rack of message cards, a telephone and a narrow order book. Rhonwen, in black, advanced from among the close-packed green pails of flowers, including hothouse carnations and smart roses.

'Don't get up. I am not wanting flowers — only to ask you a kindness. You read in the paper of the inquest on my husband, Adda? Cremated on the 18th. You made me a wreath, ordered by phone.'

'You've come to pay for it?' Blodwen offered no verbal condolences, only an automatic gravity of facial expression, brief in duration, as she took up the chicken wing again in her fingers. She had short plump thighs, visible from a scrap of frock, like the expanses of freckled bosom from which arias used to emerge full blown. 'Sit down, *cariad.*' There was a stool close by.

'I sent you a cheque the next day. Five pounds was your estimate on the phone.'

'I wonder, did I tick it off?' Blodwen reached for the grubby order book and, the full name and address supplied, said, 'Yes; a cheque from the Bedd Bowling Club came on the 25th. Coo, I wish all my customers were as quick as that. Clubs and official bodies, well, I could warn you! Quick enough in sending their own bills out.' A talker, she took her ease as, the chicken-wing bones pushed away, she fetched from a drawer of the table a paper bag and began eating chocolate cream éclairs from it. 'People order high-priced and showy wreaths, then afterwards try to forget all about it — helps them to get over their grieving perhaps. I'm too soft with them and it gets about in Melin. You'd think people wouldn't want to owe for funeral expenses, but I could tell you! More than once I've had to get my solicitor to send a warning letter. Once I had trouble with the people that ran the Horeb Music Festival — chapel deacons they were then, too — where I've sung myself in days past. They ordered a big bouquet for Trudy Skipp, who came down from London for the *Messiah*, and it was over six months before I had my money, though tickets sold as fast as farm poultry on market day.'

'I sang at the Horeb Festival once, in the chorus of *Elijah*. Free of charge, the chorus.'

'I *thought* I'd seen you somewhere . . . . Excuse a minute.' A man, who had been peering at the unpriced flowers and plants in the window, came in, asked the price of a cactus, and departed with celerity. 'Weddings are best,' Blodwen resumed, taking a second éclair. 'They seldom let you down — no grudge against paying afterwards, strangely enough. Of course I send my bills in quickly for *them*, while the good spirits last. With funerals it's more decent to wait and see if they pay without a reminder.'

'I am treasurer of the Bedd Women's Guild and a cheque for their wreath will be made out next week. It must be counter-signed by Mrs Pyle-Williams, our president.' Blodwen nodded and Rhonwen asked, 'The Gas Board paid for theirs?'

'The Gas Board? Let me see.' Blodwen re-opened the order book. 'No . . . . Six pounds.' She gave information readily. 'Something tells me *they* will be slow, like they are about sending men for repairs and leakages.' She frowned, closing the book. 'If I get trouble I'll knock six pounds off their next bill for my gas cooking.'

'All the people who ordered for my husband are in the book?'

'Yes. Some paid cash down — personal customers in the shop.'

'There was a spray of chrysanthemums with a typewritten card saying "From a friend", and no name except of your shop in the corner. I am wanting to write a letter of thanks to everyone, you see.'

Blodwen pondered for a moment, and recalled, 'Ah, I remember. A boy came here and asked for one of my cards, then came back with it typewritten, which I thought unusual myself.'

'A boy!'

Blodwen, occupied with eating, took out of the bag a third, and last, éclair. Rhonwen's exclamatory tone escaped her attention. 'A boy. I remember his thick yellow hair — oh, so yellow, though it needed a wash to bring out the real gold in it.' She dabbed at her éclair-smudged lips with a torn piece of tissue paper, and Rhonwen had time to assume her normal demeanour. 'I remember there was a boy in a concert singing *Oh for the Wings of a Dove*, and he had hair just as yellow, but washed clean the day before, I daresay.'

'You are sure it was a boy?'

'I sang at the concert myself,' Blodwen ran on heedlessly. 'In Carmarthen. I don't like boys singing solo in concerts. They always steal the show, and their parents get swollen-headed, never thinking that the voices of the little devils break and soon there won't be any more pure silver tones.'

'This boy with the typewritten card — the particulars are in your order book?'

Blodwen reached for the book, saying without effort at recall, 'When he brought the typewritten card back he told me a lady who couldn't get out wanted a sheaf of chrysanthemums sent to the undertakers and I was to post the bill to her.' She ran a finger down two pages and gave a name and address, adding, 'A nice street, and the spray wasn't dear.'

'Is it paid for?'

'Not yet. I see I posted her a bill the day after the cremation, because she was a stranger to me.'

'Will you tell me how much it was, please? I would like to pay for it.'

'Two pounds.'

Rhonwen opened her glossily new black handbag and laid two pounds on the table. 'If her cheque comes, or the boy, you will just say "Account paid" please, and not give my name.'

Assenting readily, Blodwen jotted a few words on the item in the order book, made a receipt on one of her cards, and Rhonwen stepped into the fragrant shop area. 'I've never had a cactus,' she said, and bought a prickly specimen for a pound, a recumbent protuberance like a baby marrow lying on potted miniature pebbles, but bristling with needle-sharp thorns. Blodwen gave her hints as to its care, which, the purchase being only a token of thanks, did not interest Rhonwen.

Sensing prosperity in this widow, Blodwen, still gossiping, and herself separated from a husband, said, 'Too early for you to make plans yet? Don't sit at home grieving. A lovely black suit you're wearing! I saw it in Ann Jones's window weeks ago. She's doing well, isn't she, now that she's had her shop done up?' Ann was the Melin native who now called her shop Boutique. A story ran that a cheeky Plaid Cymru young man had pushed his head into her plushy shop and shouted, 'Why don't you put a card in your window saying *Welsh spoken upstairs*?'

'I would like to open a shop in Melin,' Rhonwen said, sniffing a carnation. 'People coming in and out . . . . '

'There's premises going cheap down in St. Athan's Lane. Rates are low there too. But it's all cobbles and women don't like walking on cobbles. Superintendent Cosker's wife broke a hip falling there one wet day on her way to the police station.'

Rhonwen put her nose near an arum lily. 'You stock the best out-of-season flowers.'

'Whatever you do, don't start giving credit to customers. It gets about. I've often thought I'll have to sing for my supper again one day, on the wireless or somewhere. My agents still send me a Christmas card.'

In her car, parked at the kerbside, Rhonwen had no need to scribble the name and address on her shopping-pad. She had already known them. But she wanted to be certain. During the previous night, awake after yet another of the hauntings, it had occurred to her that the spray of chrysanthemums, with its anonymous typewritten card, could have been ordered by some other woman than this Eirene. She had remembered Insurance Evans telling her of the cause of Adda taking umbrage at being called a randy old goat by a fellow-member of the Bowling Club. Such a taunt implied a flock.

# Two

It was raining that Saturday afternoon, authoritative rain, falling with its customary announcement of a right to persist, the encircling mountain-tops crowded with their faithful assembly of swollen autumn clouds. Excellent for the local grass and therefore for the prized sheep, the rain was so familiar that nobody complained or found it depressing; smelling of the clean sky with a whiff of sea air in it, its softness washed skins and clothes advantageously. That England kept wanting more of this bounty in gigantic reservoirs, drowning whole sacred vales, was not surprising.

Rhonwen stopped her car some distance from the house she would be calling at in Camber Road. She was early for the appointment. The street trees dripped pleasantly from such russet leaves as were left on them, and the pairs of Edwardian houses on both sides looked so well-kept that any irregular activities within would not be suspected. A young woman in a mackintosh and shiny high boots passed under a green umbrella, a bag of shopping in her other hand. Another car swished through the tarmac rivulets. A gutter drain, half-choked with leaves, gurgled melodiously. People would be preparing their tea, snug in these houses whose eaves beetled darkly, a single attic window of cramped secrecy under each. It was a street suggesting bank accounts in order, where people taken ill would be cosseted, and domestic cleanliness at least was rife.

Rhonwen, a hand resting limply on the driving wheel, sat in reverie. She was recalling in particular a walk down this street, on the other side of the wide road, one afternoon a little more than a year before. The trees had been heavy with leaves then. For extra disguise, she had bought a pair of dark-tinted glasses when she had arrived at Melin by bus from Bedd. She wore a flowered new dress and also a low-brimmed hat, kept for the occasion, which Adda had never seen. This car she sat in now had been outside a house with a monkey-puzzle tree in the centre of a patch of garden, below a wide bay window. It hadn't been necessary even to turn her head to verify the car number.

A week before that walk she had gone to the Melin public library and asked to see the Electoral Register. The name she sought, with its address, was in it. Prior to that, she had found the name, but of course not the address, in a hurried run through the stubs of Adda's current cheque book, which, for once, he had left accessible in the open bureau when he had been called outside by men working on repairs to Cartref. And prior to *that*, intuition had provided messages from its dark depths — for years and years. Five, six years? Oh, longer, slowly becoming more frequent.

The summer walk down this street, the tightening of her inside when she caught sight of the car outside that house! At the end of the street she took a turning leading to the town centre and a quiet café where she lingered for over an hour. Then she returned to Camber Road, took the same walk, and there was the car still parked outside the house. She caught the five o'clock return bus to Bedd and was home in half an hour. Adda arrived a couple of hours later. These weekly absences were explained by him as 'keeping in touch' with his former Gas Board colleagues: that all such were males went without saying.

She kept her eye on the clock in the dashboard. She was not at all nervous. Determination sustained her. But what kind of woman awaited her, what nasty drama might face her? Thought of Mrs Pyle-Williams kept returning. Despite their female lack of admiration for each other, the commanding president of the Women's Guild seemed an intangible support now, much more than the image of the virtuous and helpful Insurance Evans — as a man he probably would veer way from moral support in such a matter. There was nobody to whom she could turn for sympathy and advice. She was alone. Realization of it gave her pride and strength. She had a mission.

At four-thirty she drew up at the house with the monkey-puzzle tree, slammed the car door resolutely and opened the umbrella for the few seconds' walk on a paved path and up three steps to a shallow porch and a door inset with two panels of stained glass, both depicting a heavily draped, weighty-haired woman of pensive pre-Raphaelite grace, all the leaded segments clean. She banged a knocker fixed between the panels. When the door opened, a golden-haired, large-eyed boy of seven or eight said politely, 'Please to come in'. As Rhonwen, shaking raindrops from her umbrella, stepped into the hallway, he pointed to an open door on the left. 'She's in there'. A woman's voice could be heard, apparently speaking into a telephone — 'I know how to spell that, you *twp.* It's your fault. You're always using two l's in that word . . . '

'Where can I put my umbrella?'

'Eirene puts them in that.' The boy pointed to a large earthenware ewer beyond the staircase; an umbrella already stood in it, together with a feather brush and a short-poled cleaning mop. Back there, an open door gave a glimpse of a kitchen and a room built of glass like a conservatory.

Rhonwen absorbed the whole hallway at a glance. Checked floor linoleum was polished to a gleam, a rug here and there. The carpeted staircase reached to a partitioned-off structure of glossy white plywood in which there was a closed door; the house was divided into two flats. The sturdy boy, in a jersey and shorts, closed the street door with a bang and said, 'Wet today. I'm Alcwyn'. He preceded Rhonwen into the front room. A sheathed dagger protruded from the back pocket of his bursting khaki shorts.

A rather plumply rounded woman, below average height, stood with telephone receiver in hand beside an open roll-top desk on which lay a heavy, new-looking typewriter, also several full document holders, a wad of typing paper and a box of paper tissues. Facing the entering Rhonwen, she waved her free hand in apologetic greeting, then pointed to a cane rocking chair backed with a cushion of gaudy chintz, and Rhonwen sat in it.

The room was large and high, in the Edwardian mode, suitable for the foregatherings of a growing family. A partly open door in the back wall gave sight of a bed. In the far corner beyond the fireplace stood a black sofa of worn, buttoned leather, and a folded damask screen leaning near by against the wall. In the spacious bay window stood a round table heaped with evidences of a schoolboy's hobby — small boxes of crayons, a tin of watercolour segments, paintbrushes, a jar of water and several drawing books. Alcwyn seated himself at this table, but subjected the visitor to a prolonged scrutiny. On another table at the other side of the ornate marble fireplace, lay a dish containing a freshly cut pineapple and a knife, three tea plates placed beside the odorous fruit.

'You can't have it on Tuesday,' Eirene said, after a moment of listening. 'What do you think I am — a non-stop day *and* night worker? I will phone you. A visitor has just come in. Goodbye for now.' She banged the receiver down and threw herself into a lumpily stuffed chair, which wheezed under the impact. 'He *would* phone a minute before you arrived!' she cried, on a high note of indignation. ' . . . I do typing for him,' she explained, and eyed Rhonwen more directly. 'The poet Dewi Dowdall-Jones. Fanciful language in both Welsh and English. But mostly I do straightforward business stuff that isn't flighty.'

Rhonwen wore the smart black suit bought at Ann's Boutique, a chiffon scarf of rose-pink, giving it a touch of relief, her lips lightly coated with the same tint. She looked both a mourning widow and one ready to adjust herself to any corporeal problem arising from her loss, however unpleasant. Eirene seemed to have made no concessionary effort for this afternoon's visit; her plain, short frock was slightly grubby, and also too tight for her, as though, like Alcwyn in his shorts, she had outgrown it. She could have been in her middle thirties. She was of the same racial cast as Blodwen, the florist, particularly in lack of height and her squat but agile plumpness and the strong mountain-bred legs with ability to scamper and speed. With her mass of tight, pitch-black curls, she looked altogether of Silurian ancestry, descendants of a race often seen locally. They were reputed to be highly charged in a physical sense, dionysiac, in contrast to the more puritanic Celts, usually lighter in colouring and often more religious or mystical. Rhonwen bore the Celtic aspect.

'You were surprised when I telephoned?' she began, unable to entirely conceal uneasiness at the presence of Alcwyn, at whose face she had gazed sharply.

She was then given a strange exhibition, almost in harmony with the raindrops pouring down the bay window-panes. From Eirene's eyes suddenly rushed a drenching of tears. 'My paper handkerchiefs, Alcwyn!' she cried, and the boy, without haste, got up and gave her the box of tissues from the desk. Eirene dabbed and dabbed. 'It's worse when I get excited,' she said, betraying no other evidence of stress. 'Usually it's Dewi's Welsh poems that do the harm. You see, there's something the matter with my ducts.

Brinley Richards told me we've got little bags called tear sacs, and mine get blocked like a kitchen waste-pipe, then suddenly burst in a flood without warning. I must get treatment for it some day.'

So they were not tears of grief. Rhonwen did not fidget or look impressed. Alcwyn returned to the table, trimmed a crayon with his dagger, then resumed scrutiny of Rhonwen, who said, 'Perhaps you only need glasses for your typing work.'

When the hurried gush of tears ceased, Eirene cried scoldingly to Alcwyn, 'Don't keep staring at our visitor. It's rude. Go upstairs.' She bounced out of the chair, cut a thick slice of the pineapple, laid it on a plate as the boy rose obediently, and gave it to him.

Again, Rhonwen observed him from under her lids closely. The thought had occurred to her that this boy could have been fathered by Adda. There seemed to be a mother's authority in the way unmarried Eirene addressed him and in her playful slap of his behind as, telling him to close the door, he went past her. But he had no physical resemblance to either her or Adda. Neither was there an intuitive message that an Adda offspring was in this house of misdoing.

Her rejection of the suspicion, though rather uncertain, seemed to be justified by Eirene. 'Son of the couple living upstairs,' she said, when the door closed. 'Only his father living with him there now, though. Not much good in *him*. He went to Swansea on his motorbike today, football and drinking. Alcwyn's mother has gone to Brynawel, poor thing. She was taken there last January.'

'Brynawel!' Rhonwen repeated subduedly. It was the county's institution for mental cases. People rarely said that a woman or man had been taken to an asylum; it was usually 'Gone to Brynawel'. The sombre old buildings behind high walls had been renovated and much enlarged a few years ago; visitors to its inmates did not vent harsh criticisms of it now; but still, it was seldom referred to openly as a lunatic asylum.

'She had a bad time with him,' Eirene pointed to the ceiling. 'I don't mean with Alcwyn. With his father. But her trouble had been in her family too. It would come and go with her. When they took her, the last thing she said to me was, "Look after Alcwyn".'

'So you've divided the house into two, then?' Rhonwen said,

although she already knew of the division and also what it had cost.

'The house was on the market cheap. But it was too big for just little me, and Hughes, the building people, divided it for me . . . very reasonable price too.'

'I don't like rocking chairs.' Rhowen got up restlessly. 'Makes me feel they're for grannies.' She took an upholstered chair similar to Eirene's. Her movements were those of a person with rights in this house. Actually she liked rocking chairs. But it was time to display some inkling of firmness.

'I'll get the tea,' Eirene declared, not noticing anything out of place in the abrupt change of chairs and Rhonwen's bolt upright posture. She left the room with a bouncing roll natural to her and somehow in harmony with her rounded bosom and even her mass of curly hair.

Rhonwen sat back. She had imagined the reception of herself would be different; had even expected truculence or at least coldness; not this unhostile acceptance of her visit. When she had telephoned Eirene four days days before, announcing herself as Adda's widow, there was a pause before the woman said, like anybody else, 'I was sorry to read in the papers that he had gone'. At the caller's request to visit her there was another pause, and then, readily, 'I am free on Saturday afternoon. Come to tea at four o'clock.'

Eirene returned, carrying without effort an enormous tray laden with everything needed for solid refreshment in what could still be a cruel occasion: a large teapot and an ewer of hot water, a plate of thickly buttered bread, white and brown, two pots of jam, a dish of shop pastries in frilled containers and, unexpectedly, a stout glass jar of pickled onions that did not suggest purchase in a shop.

'Rain's in for all the weekend, I expect.' Eirene brought to the visitor's chair a low table from a nest of them. 'You would like a slice of pineapple?' This refused, Eirene poured cups at the window table and went to and fro offering edibles. 'I'll call Alcwyn down for his tea a bit later on,' she said. Was it a hint that Rhonwen was not expected to remain long? Seating herself, she went on, 'I've got a lot of work on hand just now. They bring me mixed up papers to type and picking a way through them is hell. I often think they're the cause of my tear sacs blocking up, besides Dewi's long Welsh poems.'

'You earn your living at typing?'

'Yes. I do regular work for some small business men, and a lot of private people bring me letters . . . Dewi,' she rambled on, 'lives in this street. He's not married and he never stops writing at weekends and in evenings when he's home from his teaching job in the Comprehensive. Every year he hopes to win the Chair or Crown at the National Eisteddfod competition. I dread his work in Welsh. I can speak home Welsh, but in writing or print I get muddled.' She cut herself a slice of pineapple, and resumed, 'Sometimes I think I ought to have kept my job at the Gas Board'.

Rhonwen blinked at this piece of news. 'You worked for the Gas Board?'

'Oh yes. For eight years. I went there soon as I left a secretarial school in Swansea.' Attentive to her visitor's wants, Eirene asked, 'You would like an onion with your bread and butter?'

'No, thank you.' Rhonwen's aspect of powers held in reserve was still paramount in this tittle-tattle.

'I pickle them myself. Adda used to like them with his tea.'

The tiny bomb, miniature as the onions in their spiced vinegar, exploded mildly enough. Perhaps Eirene too only wanted shilly-shallying to end, but it was still too sudden for Rhonwen, who wanted to be the first to dart into real matters, in her own way. She merely remarked, 'I never knew him eat pickled onions.'

Eirene's dark, dark eyes darted a momentarily suspicious glance at this restrained woman, but her manner remained equable as she took another plunge. 'Slipping on a cliff like that! Was he looking for gulls' eggs? Do they lay in the autumn?'

'I don't know when they lay.' For the first time Rhonwen sounded impatient.

'I remember my Auntie Gwen telling me about a neighbour's boy who went looking for gulls' eggs up in those wild parts. Had to be rescued from a ledge. Policemen and ropes. Some foreigner tramping up there heard him crying. Ceri, the boy's name. Same age as myself. He's an engine driver on the railways now.'

Rhonwen laid her half-finished cup down. Why had she consented to take tea in this house? Eirene was scatter-brained.

'I've come here about my husband,' she declared.

Eirene gulped over a swallowed piece of pineapple. 'What is it you want to know?'

'He visited here once a week over several years.' It was a flat statement, not a question.

'Not the same day every week,' Eirene declared, candid if obscure in point. 'Sometimes, when Wednesday suited me better than Thursday, he'd go to some bowling club he belonged to.' Her hand plucked at a string of beads lying down her frank exposure of lightly tanned bosom.

All pretence of continuing with the tea victuals was abandoned. Rhonwen became another woman in demeanour. The lower part of her face seemed twice its normal size, and remorselessly hard. Her other self had risen out of the depths. Her lips drew together, and from the gathered aperture her voice issued with a low dangerous sibilance, which yet avoided a spitting fury. 'You wicked woman!'

'I'm not,' cried Eirene shrilly, 'I'm not a wicked woman.'

'You killed my husband.'

Shrillness rose higher. 'I didn't; I didn't. How do you mean, I killed him?'

'He committed suicide.' The clarity of the measured words rang out. 'Because of you.'

Eirene's bow-shaped mouth kept wide open for seconds before an amount of self-control gained on her. 'The inquest on him said he slipped accidentally down Pen Mawr cliff! It was in the paper!' She was struggling valiantly to cope, and half failing — a wailing run in her voice betrayed that. She too knew there was a world of misleading, vague, public pronouncements and a private world of true knowledge. Here in her house was a woman who possibly could ruin her socially in Melin, even if revelation could humiliate its revealer too.

Rhonwen took breath. 'I was his wife. I lived with him all the time he knew you, and I saw him going to pieces. Shame ate at him. He was brought up strictly by one of the most respected families for miles around. He had a daughter he was proud of. He — '

'Stop! Stop!' Eirene cried. She pressed her chubby hands over her ears.

'I won't stop. He married me and everything was right until you came into his life. He retired from the Gas Board before his time. Why? Not because his father left him money — and I expect you knew about that money — a lot of it spent on you — but because he could see you easier and more often, with plenty of time on his hands. More time for your wickedness. He — '

'It's not true! Only once a week coming here!'

Rhonwen ignored the futile interruption. 'He set you up in this house. That's why you left the Gas Board.' She cast a look of contempt at the roll-top desk; 'Made you *seem* a worker in your own business. He bought you that typewriter at Watkins in February last year. It cost seventy pounds.'

'My old one was falling to pieces. I work hard on low pay and some bills outstanding. The poet owes me fifteen pounds. And there's . . .'

Rhonwen would not be side-tracked. 'I have all Adda's papers now,' she emphasized. 'They were kept locked up by him until his suicide. Bank statements and cheque stubs going back for many years. Seven years ago he bought this house for you — cheap, it's true, though not so cheap for the time; its value today is double or more the four thousand he paid. Then he paid Hughes three hundred and eighty-five pounds for the division into two flats, so that rent could be drawn from a tenant. Did you give him that rent as interest on all he had spent? Did you, did you? Of course you didn't. I calculate he spent at least ten thousand pounds on you over the years, and I am the sufferer.' A spot of red had come to both cheeks. She was obliged to halt the tirade.

Eirene, in a brief access of extraordinary sagacity, asked: 'Why didn't he destroy those old cheque stubs and bank statements? Did he want you to see them after his death?'

Counter-attacked though she was by this unexpected taunt, Rhonwen parried, 'How would he know he'd die before me? He was worried and eaten by shame, but that doesn't kill a man.'

'You said he committed suicide.'

'People often commit suicide on sudden impulse,' Rhonwen shot back without pause. 'Adda kept old business papers because it was trained into him, head clerk that he was at the Gas Board. For years he drew regular sums of cash from his current account at the bank and they could only have been for you. You bled him, and at last he committed suicide.'

Eirene's underswell of wailing burst through fully for a moment. 'He enjoyed himself here! He didn't commit suicide because of me; I didn't drive him to it even if he did it. He enjoyed himself here.' On a lower key, emotion abating, she said, almost in a confidential way such as neighbours employ over a garden wall, 'He used to beat me.'

'*Beat* you?' Rhonwen was totally arrested.

'Not hard.' Self-justification seemed to come. 'I'm weak by nature and I never preached at him, and he didn't do my bottom any harm.' Eirene added, 'He just had his fancies.' No statement issuing from her shocked but reduced visitor, she resumed, in a philosophical way, woman to woman, 'That's how they are, aren't they? This and that. All the year round. We've got to put up with them.'

'You deserved it.' Rhonwen spoke in a low voice. It was as though she had not heard Eirene's impudent remarks suggestive of a wife's association with such practices.

'He saw an old feather brush in the kitchen that I was going to throw away. You know how the feathers drop out one by one, moulting until there's only three or four left to brush away spiders' webs and dust on the window sills. "Just the thing," he said when I told him I was going to buy a new one, and he tore the last feathers from the cane.'

There was no evidence of calculated retaliation in these candid reminiscences, but as she finished Eirene sustained another attack from her faulty tear ducts. The drops flowed out unstinted, laving her cheeks, falling to the freckled space of flesh bared in her tight, v-necked frock and vanishing into her dusky cleavage. 'Where's my tissues?' she cried, apparently blinded by the strange gush. Rhonwen not getting up to fetch the box from where it lay flung on the desk after the previous drenching, Eirene stumbled for it herself and dabbed and wiped, slightly gasping. It seemed believable that emotion — of deep-buried guilt? — emptied those tear sacs.

'You want treatment,' Rhonwen advised coldly.

'They all say that.' Eirene sat back, still gasping a little. She applied hand-pressure to her breasts, which indeed appeared to have swollen.

The rain thrashed on the window panes. Rhonwen waited a few more seconds for Eirene's attack to subside, then proceeded, 'I haven't finished yet.'

'Did he make a will?'

Rhonwen treated this further impudence as something to be expected and borne from such a woman. 'Yes. I inherit what is left after his extravagance with you.'

'You mustn't say that I drove him to suicide,' Eirene pleaded.

'You did not think *you* would be a legatee in the will, did you? Not after all the cash he drew for you. I've put the amounts down on three sheets of paper at home, copied from his cheque book stubs over the years.'

'I don't drink and I seldom smoke,' Eirene declared, going off at a tangent again. 'I don't dress up. I haven't got jewellery of any worth.'

'There's this house.'

Eirene's face twitched. Was there going to be another downfall of tears, so soon after the last? Her hand fidgeted at the box of tissues on her robust lap. She peered, still a little glaucous, at Rhonwen. She was apprehending the threat floating in the air. A timidity came. 'The house was for me and bought in my name.'

'The cheques for the purchase money and sundry connecting matters were signed by Adda. I am a widow. Adda's pension from the Gas Board stopped at his death. I help our struggling daughter and her two children and sick husband in Australia. Why should I scrimp and do without? I might have to sell my home.'

'What are you meaning?'

'I want the ownership deeds of this house transferred to me.'

Eirene's immediate reaction was trivial. 'I can't afford a motor car!' Beyond the streaming window panes and the monkey-puzzle tree in the neat patch of turf the car stood at the kerb, as it had on countless afternoons. The trapped culprit, gazing vacantly at the streaked panes, seemed bereft of further speech. She was given a minute for the fiat to be assimilated. Then she mumbled, 'Adda gave the house to me.'

'Well, his lawful widow wants it included in his estate.'

Was there a hint of legal action, however forlorn its chances of success? Was it blackmail? Or merely a compulsion to inflict punishment? Eirene did not shrink or seem daunted. For the moment she was only confused at being thus brought up smartly to heel for conduct that still was disgracefully reprehensible in a place like Melin, where, memories being long and well-rooted in puritan soil, it would not be easily condoned or forgotten by most people. She might lose typing business because of it; she had not the vision or calculation to foresee that equally it might increase business from some quarters, probably male. Rhonwen sat waiting. No hatred was manifest in her. Neither did she suggest a cat amusing itself with a mouse.

'You mean you would go to law?'

'That must be thought about.'

A glimmering came into Eirene's eyes. 'You would drag his name down.'

'And yours with it, my girl.'

'I'm not a wicked woman,' Eirene cried, 'I'm not, I'm not.'

Rhonwen brought her back firmly to the subject under business dispute. 'You are drawing rent from the tenant upstairs. If neither you nor he can be turned out of this house under the present Rent Acts, I would expect to be paid his rent, and rent from you too.'

'I must go to a solicitor.' Panic ran high in Eirene's voice. She was of those who hold solicitors, with their violations of privacies, in dread.

Taking a lace-edge handkerchief from her new handbag, expensive as the suit she had bought with it at the Boutique, Rhonwen blew her nose with a sound as delicate as her body seemed to be. 'Solicitors welcome business from high or low,' she remarked. 'They're apt to ask awkward questions, and certainly they can turn out to be costly — speaking the truth often is.'

A sharp rat-tatting of the door knocker must have resounded throughout the house. Eirene made no move. She was still mesmerized by her dilemma. 'I expect it's only Dewi Dowdall-Jones, the poet. He knocks like that. He'll go away.'

'I can give you time to think about it all,' Rhonwen proceeded, in a concluding way and shutting the clasp of her handbag decisively, a woman in command of this situation. Herself inconsequent, she said, 'I collected Adda's ashes at the crematorium yesterday'.

'What are you going to do with them?' Eirene asked, glad of the respite.

'Scatter them in the garden of our house, I think; Cartref, my home and Adda's.'

No sound of pattering footsteps was heard, but the door into the hall opened, and Alcwyn burst in, followed by a hesitant man. 'I want my tea,' Alcwyn shouted. He gave Rhonwen a stare of mingled impatience and alarm.

Eirene now accepted the interruption with relief. 'Go to the table and eat cakes.' She introduced the hovering man to Rhonwen. The youngish poet was saturnine, his face handsome in an uneven way, petulant-lipped, hauteur around his nostrils, though his air of brooding melancholy was attractive and made him seem sound of judgment. 'I told you on the phone it isn't quite ready yet,' Eirene said as he sat down. 'I'll work on it tomorrow, Sunday though it is.' She turned to Rhonwen. 'Dewi is itching to win the Chair or the Crown at the National with a long poem,' she repeated. Over at the window table, Alcwyn began to devour the plate of untouched shop pastries, poured himself cold tea into Eirene's cup and pulled a face when he took a sip of it.

'I've brought you another one to type,' Dewi said, taking a folded sheet of paper from his pocket. 'Short and in English. I wrote it this morning after Elwyn Roberts' coffin was delivered to his house next door to my lodgings . . . . You knew Elwyn Roberts?' he asked Rhonwen politely, and she shook her head but wondered where she had seen the poet before. 'Age ninety-two. Four married daughters. They've arrived at his house today and you can hear their loud voices quarrelling through the wall.' He unfolded the sheet, took out a pencil, and made a correction.

'Don't stuff yourself with *all* those pastries, Alcwyn,' Eirene scolded. 'You'll be taken bad.'

'Surely you gave a talk once to the Women's Guild at Bedd, Mr Dowdall-Jones?' Rhonwen inquired. 'Subject, a traveller of bygone times.'

'Giraldus Cambrensis. They wouldn't have the talk in Welsh, I remember.'

'I am treasurer and secretary of the Guild. Mrs Pyle-Williams is president. She favours Welsh, but over seventy per cent of members are against it for Guild talks.' The influential name of the president was brought in deliberately; a cohort of reputable women lay behind it. Eirene rocked and rocked in her chair.

The poet eyed her as she rocked, her thick legs apart in the short frock, displaying the stretched tops of stockings as the chair swung up. She was deeply preoccupied. It was not in her disposition to mope, and her face became stodgy now from lack of animation. Was it to divert her or dissipate the strained atmosphere in the room that he asked if her could read his new English poem — 'It's in a free form,' he assured them. 'That old Welsh metre the Eisteddfod demands for the Bardic Chair competition is an iron corset on a man. They call it *awdl.* It's the one you're typing, Eirene *fach.*' His look at her was fond.

'Read the English one if you want,' she said, not consulting Rhonwen, who glanced from him to her. How far did their association go?

'You will let me read it?' the poet asked the visitor, who of course could not refuse. Over at the window table Alcwyn slumped heavily in his chair, picking his nose; he might have endured such readings on other occasions.

In his light, silvery voice, a contrast to the Hamlet gloom of his face, the poet recited pleasantly:

*Elwyn Roberts Next Door*

The rain falls today, each drop a stranger to the others.
An oak coffin slides into the house next door.
There a man died of old, old age,
Speaking little sense for two years, not knowing his daughters.
He gave me a goldfish for my tank, dahlias from his garden.

All of us are goldfish in a glass tank,
Strangers, circling round and round.
They flick a tail at neighbours coming too near,
Or is it a message, a strawberry-red tail sending a telegram,
A language of fish, saying

Stranger you will die like me, and this water will not
miss you,
You cannot grab my tail, we will circle forever alone . . .
Fish, fish, flick me a telegram from your tail,
Remembering him.

Eirene stopped rocking. 'You've still got your tank of goldfish then, same as Elwyn had? I never met his daughters. Are they cremating him? Ask for the rest of his fish. You were as good to him as the Welfare people. Grab the tails of those fish, Dewi.'

The poet handed her the manuscript of his poem. 'Six carbon copies,' he ordered extravagantly.

Alcwyn reared up, exhibiting hysteria. He banged his flat hand on the table several times. 'I want a cup of hot tea,' he shouted. His eyes flashed, his yellow hair swung over his forehead, his body swelled with indignation. Did the outburst hold a hereditary trace of his mother's derangement?

Rhonwen took advantage of the disturbance and rose to leave. She had deposited her own explosive. 'Well, best wishes for winning the Chair or Crown next August,' she told the poet courteously. 'Perhaps you will address the Bedd Women's Guild again some time. I will mention your poems to Mrs Pyle-Williams. She goes to the Eisteddfod every year and I daresay knows all the Gorsedd members and adjudicators.' Not that it had ever been discovered that back-scene favouritism could affect the competitive events in the great week-long annual gathering to celebrate the pure arts, its circle of druid-gowned leaders stainless, whatever they were like in their worldly professions.

Eirene ushered her to the front door, fetching the umbrella. She said nothing. But in her eyes, in her nostrils, ears, in every attribute of her body, seemed to lay an instinctive suspicion she could not as yet formulate. An alarming situation had been created by this visit, and whether it could be resolved was not to be foreseen. Had the widow appeased a natural fury in her visit and would retire satisfied with exercise of her tongue this afternoon? Were the threats and fiats genuine?

Rhonwen turned on the top porch step. 'I will be phoning you again,' she said, and, opening her umbrella, added, 'I have paid Blodwen the florist for the spray you sent to Adda's funeral.'

She drove slowly through the full-dropping rain, preoccupied as Eirene had been in the rocking chair. That poet had said a true thing in his poem. People went round and round alone in a glass tank of their fellows just the same as goldfish. Nobody achieved real identification with anyone else. The interview with Eirene had verified what she had thought during the last few years of Adda's life — he had become a complete stranger weary of her. At the same time she rejected admittance of the conclusion in its entirety. She adjusted it to a realization — and it helped to ease the guilt lurking in her vitals — that Adda was a secret rascal who had cheated and robbed her. Nevertheless, there had been the earlier years of satisfying union, fulfilment as far as such could be achieved. But the great rewarding unison of late married life, the peace that reigns supreme over petty disputes, had not come.

The peculiar thing was that she felt an elusive touch of liking for Eirene. She had expected to meet a calculating dressed-up hussy who had ensnared a man during a dangerously weakened period in his life, leading him astray, bleeding him of money, drinking a lot of gin, lavish with cosmetics. Now she felt that Eirene had not demanded purchase of the house or wheedled other expenditures. Adda was the real culprit, if only in humbug and weakness. It was to help pay for the house and its owner that he had become eccentrically mean at home and — it was her main obsession — kept dodging the promised cruise to Australia, a trip which also would have deprived him of his pleasures with Eirene for many weeks.

But the woman could have driven him out of her life, couldn't she? She knew she was filching from his wife not only money, but the other, more important thing, the treasury of bondage in marriage. She let him beat her. Anger and horror returned. Pandering to him! Rhonwen's blood rose as she imagined the provocative scene — a naked bottom and her husband wielding the cane of a feather brush. Worse, the thought even occurred to her that he might have imagined he was thus punishing his wife for his long shackling to her. She increased speed through the rhythmic rain. As her thoughts hurled on, she granted honesty and frankness to Eirene. In a way, they were allies. Then the thought came that Eirene held a trump card. If, in retaliation for loss of her house, she chose to be courageous and reveal to others that Adda indulged in that thrashing vice, his wife's existence in Bedd would become a matter of stealthy gossip, fingers pointed, unseemly mirth in pubs. In a land given to nicknames, surnames being so few, she might earn one such as Rhonwen Feather Brush. A member of the Women's Guild had long been known, off and on, as Olwen Wellington Boot after she was seen kicking her husband out of their house into a flooded road.

Inferences and deductions in confusion, yet still upheld by a justification of the afternoon's mission, she put the car away, but remained in her seat, hands on the wheel, and listened to the rain beating on the garage roof. Dusk was gathering. Why didn't she want to make the effort to go into the house? An impulse came to back the car out again, go for a long journey. Where to? A cinema in Swansea? Take a meal in a restaurant? Even spend the night in a hotel? Why did her mind return to that poet? He had a mysterious aura. She would have liked to talk to him alone. He had reminded her of a youngish chapel preacher she met in her girlhood, when he came to Bedd as a stop-gap while Parch. Watcyn Watcyns was in hospital for a gall-stone operation. They had the same streak of lonely melancholy, stirring an urge to protect and nourish.

She looked about her restlessly, unable to come to a decision. She could see on a shelf beside the car, among various objects kept there, such as a lidless casserole, a bag of bulbs and a box of tools, the round casket of fake copper that contained Adda's ashes. After collecting it from the crematorium, and paying a fee, she had opened it for a moment in the garage, and the strange, gritty, dully phosphorescent heap within had meant nothing. Vaguely she knew that she would not scatter the contents in the garden or remove the casket from that shelf yet.

Inertia prevented her from driving out again for a trip. She could barely open the car door. All that had happened these last weeks had reached a culmination point that afternoon, and it had worn her out. Nerves of steel could suddenly snap and turn as slack as wool. She felt that a bad night awaited her. But her supply of sleeping tablets on prescription had been renewed at the chemist's in Bedd on the way back from the crematorium the day before.

One foot out of the car, her attention was caught by something moving swiftly on the shadowy wall below the shelf. A huge cockroach! Descending from under the shelf, its wide glossy back looking strong as a carapace, it was a black creature of extraordinary dimensions for a cockroach. She stared in unreasonable fear. Then suddenly it wasn't on the wall, although its scuttling had not been of such express speed that she couldn't follow its progress; it was as if the powerful thing had been absorbed into the shadowy brick wall. She had never before seen a beetle in the house or in the adjacent lean-to garage. Galvanized a little, she stepped carefully out of the car, scrutinizing the concrete floor. That living black creature had been so glossily fat that it exuded a right to be anywhere. She would never have been able to kill it. Hastening out, she slammed and locked the pair of doors, then, hastening back on the wet gravelled path, unlocked and left one door wide open.

That night she closed and fastened every window in the house, bolted front and back doors, but did not return to the garage to shut and lock it up. There had never been a burglary in Bedd, or even sneak thieves, only poaching of trout and salmon in the river, recognised from ancient times as a marginal exclusion from the Eighth Commandment, and always successful in the additional Thou Shalt Not Be Found Out. She went to bed early after a light supper. Glass of water and bottle of tablets were ready on the table under the lamp. She read a book selected at random from Adda's small collection downstairs. But she couldn't concentrate on *The Pickwick Papers*. The bulky cockroach haunted her. Had it really been there? Its size was so unreal, a tremendous ruler of all beetles, a monarch of its kingdom, scuttling out of a nasty fairy tale.

Dropping the book, she told herself she needed a change. Should she go for a week to familiar Torquay? Alone? She'd think about it tomorrow. Swallowing a tablet and half the water, she hesitated, and took another tablet; she deserved two after that crucial day. The light switched off, she lay waiting in the pleasant dark, slipping into its purple shades, yielding to the luxury of an expensive mattress which, a couple of years before, after much dispute with cheeseparing Adda, had replaced the old-fashioned kind stuffed with feathers to which he had been accustomed from his childhood. The cockroach had slipped down a chink, was no more; the dark ate it. Vague thought of Torquay returned, became vaguer, was replaced by shapeless, unknown Australia, where parrots talked Welsh . . . .

Galloping thuds came down a mist-wreathed mountainside, drew nearer, and out of the mist towards her came the red-horned ram, faintly evident at first, then, in unison with the louder thudding of hoof, his evil head charged nearer to where she stood rooted in an agony of rigidity. His jaw held a walking stick, its silver band distinct below the curved handle. In the split second before impact she woke.

'*Iesu Mawr!*' she cried, invoking the Saviour's name immediately she realized that she had not been smashed to pieces. A coma of her legs had dominated the nightmare. Relief succeeded the fright. She switched the light on and saw by her watch that it was only half past five. She could dimly remember that there had been other dreams, but could not connect any of the preceding ones with that sense of destructive hoofs galloping out horribly from mist. She blamed the polluting sleeping tablets. There must be other kinds which did not unlock such gates of hell. She'd call on Dr Llewellyn on Monday.

Going downstairs in her dressing gown to prepare a cup of soothing malted milk, she told herself, 'Yes, a week in Torquay is what you want, *cariad.*' The milk heated and drunk, and a promise of dawn already greying the kitchen window, an access of energy came. She would not return to bed. She cast about for a job to accomplish and her eye fell on the pair of brass scales. It had not been polished for . . . how long? Not since the week she had gone picking blackberries and weighed them for the bramble-jelly preparations.

She tied an apron round her dressing gown and sat at the newspaper-covered table with the scales, cloths and a canister of liquid polish. The smooth pair of shallow bowls, perfectly balanced despite their shop use since Victorian days, always pleased her. The wide mahogany base required a beeswax polish.

Its slotted row of weights, flat-bottomed and stamped, ranging from two pounds to a toy-like half an ounce, did not gleam so lustrously as the tall spine and its delicately balancing arms from which chains held the bowls of fine brass. She polished and polished. Dawn came as usual to the window. She was glad the rain still fell, an activity of beneficence. She went into the hall to open the front door and admit the refreshing air of day. But the door was already off the latch and open an inch.

She stood before it, as rooted to the ground as in her nightmare. She clearly remembered locking and bolting the door, her last activity before going up to bed. An intruder had broken in somewhere and left by the front door! Or was he still hiding in the house? She returned to the kitchen, found its door into the back garden locked and bolted, the window-catch undisturbed. Fearless, she went into all the rooms, examining windows, opening cup-board and wardrobes, looking under beds, almost certain all the time that nobody would be found. There was no evidence that anything had been disturbed. Her father's walking stick was in its usual place in the hall stand. The thought struck her that she had walked in her sleep. Her mind had been thoroughly disturbed in a violent upheaval of her faculties.

Had the visit to Eirene achieved all that? She brushed the thought aside, blaming the double dose of tablets in a growing certainty that she had walked in her sleep. She threw a mackintosh over her dressing gown, took her umbrella, and hastened through the rain to the garage. The door she had left open was shut, and the pair was locked; she ran back to the house, found the Yale key was still in her handbag, returned to the garage, unlocked the door, peeped in. Of course the car was there. Was that monster cockroach still there too?

When she had returned to the kitchen, and stood among its familiarities, her beloved scales gleaming on the table, she attempted to lay the mystery aside. If she had walked to the garage in her sleep wouldn't her nightdress have been drenched with rain? But perhaps the rain had stopped for a while? She shook off possible solutions. The mystery was part of that nightmare, and best kept at a distance in another domain. She went upstairs, took a hot bath, dressed, boiled an egg, made toast and coffee, and resolutely began to think of a resumption of her duties as treasurer and secretary of the W.G.

Realizing it was Sunday, she even contemplated going down to the village to attend chapel, which she had not done for a year or more. Yes, she would go to the eleven o'clock service. The decision brought a firmer sense of normal reality. She busied herself in the kitchen, preparing the Sunday joint, half a shoulder of lamb, trimming it of fat, sticking rosemary here and there in the mild red of the local meat. She fetched mint from the back garden to chop and soak in vinegar while she was in chapel.

Soon after ten the telephone rang. She was glad to hear the peremptory sound. She half-expected the caller to be Insurance Evans. It was Eirene. At first it seemed she had rung merely to apologise for the interruption of their talk yesterday by the poet's arrival. This preliminary did not deceive Rhonwen, who said she intended recommending the poet for another W.G. talk. Then Eirene said, 'I have had a bad night. Worrying and worrying. Up early before it was light.' It was almost like a friend of long standing confiding bosom to bosom.

'You must ask your doctor for sleeping tablets.'

'I sleep like a log as a rule. Nothing the matter with me as a rule. Take things as they come as a rule. But last night I left my bed at 5 o'clock. Someone seemed to be in the room, pacing about in the dark. Couldn't get off. So I dressed and gave myself something to do. I cooked the leg of lamb that Alcwyn and his father will be coming down to share with me at one o'clock as usual on Sundays. I do it for the sake of Alcwyn, not his father. A whole leg of lamb. I'll heat it up for them. Alcwyn's father pays me more than half of what I spend on the Sunday joint and vegetables, and I must say he's regular with his rent too, a no-good man though he is in most respects . . . .' The rambling, with its hint of jumpiness, paused.

'I'm having lamb too. Half a shoulder.' Judicious, herself playing for time, Rhonwen added, 'I'm just chopping mint from the garden. Then I'm going to chapel.'

'I'm not giving them mint sauce. Forgot about it, and no mint in my garden. They — '

'If you were awake all night did you think about what I want?

The house deeds, your tenant's rent and rent from you, backdated to your occupancy?'

Eirene's voice rose from its jerky attempts at gossiping chatter. 'But Adda didn't put all that in his will, did he?' The blunt retaliatory question was nervous.

'You know very well there are rights besides the things in wills. I am claiming my rights as Adda's widow, sole legatee of all his possessions. Public opinion would be on my side.'

Something like a half-choked outburst of sounds came. Was Eirene having one of her floods of tears? Rhonwen waited, her free hand rearranging Michaelmas daisies in a vase on the hall table, beside the telephone. She was almost certain that Eirene would never go to law or seek advice in this very private matter, with its revelation of the wages of sin, and possibly including a courageous revelation of the feather brush. A daisy stem broke in Rhonwen's hand. Would she herself have the courage to face the social débacle in Bedd? At the moment she thought she would. The scandal might even prove to be enjoyable; and, after all, she was not too old to disappear to Australia for ever after this business was settled. Adda's own reputation would not matter any longer. A casket of ashes was of no account.

Eirene said, in a subdued way, 'The house is in my name in the deeds.'

'That could be contested. I tell you, an innocent, good-living widow would get the sympathy of all right-minded people . . . . Look,' she went on, resolution suddenly achieved, 'I will arrange another meeting with you.'

'I can't settle to typing,' Eirene wailed. 'That Dewi from down the road is bullying me to finish his long Welsh poem that he's submitting for the next Eisteddfod. It's driving me mad. I couldn't work at it yesterday, after he had gone, and he won't pay me a penny until it is finished — and then he'll pay in dribs and drabs, taking advantage of me. He — ' She seemed about to launch into more chatterbox loquacity, as if tears had abated.

'Look, I am preparing to go to chapel and can't stop any longer. Goodbye now. I will phone one day soon.' Let the taste of adulteress' torment be prolonged. The telephone receiver was laid down with satisfaction.

Yet the satisfaction was not truly vindictive. Going upstairs to change into her mourning black, she experienced again the peculiar feeling of intimate and even pleasurable identification with Eirene. There was a hard saying — was it in the Bible? — 'An eye for an eye, a tooth for a tooth'. But that could make life richer, be a nourishing bond between two combatants. Duels need not be fatal. As she slipped into a skirt of fine moire, a suspicion came that Eirene had encouraged and enjoyed the shocking caning of her bottom, in addition to reaping material benefit from it. Let her have another kind of punishment now. Let each of those lashes cost her a pound or two. Tit-for-tat.

Balance restored, the disorder of the night gone, she took out the car and had no further thought of the beetle or the possibility that somehow it might have climbed into the car. Neither did she wonder why she felt a compulsion to go to chapel, after the prolonged lapse. She and Adda had always continued to pay their membership dues and other contributions. It was in the chapel that they had first become aware of each other in a courtship sense, he on the left section of the narrow, full gallery running along three sides of the blue-washed edifice, she on the right. Up there, the chapel's younger members sat and dominated the hymn-singing, strong voices in full, more or less, virginal dash. That custom was almost gone now. The last time she went to chapel the sparse congregation, and nobody in the gallery, was depressing, the perfunctory sermon, mumbled prayers and slack hymn-singing yielding little other response in her.

She arrived a few minutes late at the sturdy building, erected in mid-Victorian times and still looking as if it would last for ever, like mercy and forgiveness in parts of the scriptures. She slipped into a pew at the deserted back. Her family pew, where her grandparents and parents had sat and which had a strip of worn but thick carpet on its hard seat, was down near the front. There were not more than thirty worshippers, and in the deacons' long seat below the imposing pulpit were only four men, elderly and dutiful. Parch. Watcyn Watcyns in the pulpit was old too, and his sermon plain and lack-lustre. Where was the flame of yesteryear, that came from the blood and belly and mounted to the inspirational fire of *hwyl*?

She asked herself why she had come. The urge to come here, as to a former security, had already lost force. In the middle of the sermon, she wanted to leave. Her mind could fasten on nothing of consequence for long. But she lacked the courage to rise while the preacher stood up there uttering words that had no meaning for her; he would have seen her creeping out even from this shadowy place under the back gallery. A trance began to hold her mind. Her eyelids kept drooping and lifting. Then she saw, along the narrow hymn-book shelf before her, a little beetle running, a child of that other one, but equally fast, and black-clad as herself. It vanished under the shelf-edge. She lifted her feet a few inches, kept them up a minute, then, without calculation of her action, rose quickly and went out by the adjacent door.

In the lobby she remembered that she had left her umbrella in the iron fixture attached, with its drip-pan, to the end of the pew. But she did not return to fetch it. There was only a short forecourt to traverse to reach her car. The rain pelted. She sat inert at the driving wheel for several minutes. Three or four people under umbrellas went by on the pavement. Then a man stopped and touched the peak of his waterproof cap. It was Insurance Evans, his red, solid face smiling a greeting. She wound the window down at once.

'Nice drop of rain, Rhonwen! How are you keeping now, all alone up there in Cartref?'

'You want a lift somewhere?'

'No. Only going to the Einion Arms. Ben wants to see me in his private quarters about a little business matter.' As a six-day pub, the front door would be locked all Sunday, but a bunch of trusted habitués were not allowed to feel forlorn in the morning or evening, as everybody, including P.C. Vaughan, knew. 'I like a trot in the rain. Not worth while taking my car out.' Evans lifted the sleeve of his oilskin and displayed Adda's gold watch on his wrist. 'It's going like new one. Doesn't lose time or gain. Been admired at the Bowling Club. Best present I've ever had.'

'You helped me more than anyone.'

There was a shifting of hesitancy across his straightforward face. 'Anything you want done in the house, advice or a job, don't forget I'm a handy man, Rhonwen. Bought myself an electric drill and a bag of tools at the auction sale in Careg Castle . . . . ' The uncertainty of her was still there; still she was an unassessed quantity. 'Roof of Cartref not leaking in this rain? I fixed a loose slate on a neighbour's roof the other day. Winter's coming. The blizzards and the cold.'

The impulse to ask him to share her joint of lamb passed; it might be misconstrued. She drove home at speed. There, changed from the sixty pounds Boutique suit into an everyday frock and an old well-liked cardigan, the Sunday morning became of turning-point importance. She went to one of the sideboard cupboards to which she had moved the bottles Insurance Evans had thought fit to install for possible visitors during and after Adda's obsequies. It was a bottle of brandy, three-quarters full, that she took out. Brandy was connected with medicinal reliefs. She found a cut-glass goblet of ceremonial size and antique value, which had belonged to Adda's family and was never used in her time; she washed and polished it, filled a jug with water, returned to the living room, and drew to the window the lounge chair Adda had always sat in, the one on the right side of the hearth.

She had not often taken alcohol at home. A daily glass or two of wine at the Torquay hotel she and Adda had patronized for years did not count, but she had always enjoyed those petty venturings into drink and appreciated the ensuing comfort and release. She poured a substantial measure of brandy, watered it to double, and sipped not only with a sense of adventure but of need. She liked the taste of brandy, but would have preferred champagne, with its lively sparkle and settling of gay froth, its look of clear innocence, its ready kindling of good will. How could she order champagne? Not from the Einion Arms. She'd go to the off-licence shop in Melin. Order a dozen bottles by phone tomorrow? Would they have a delivery van? It was unlikely to be seen drawn up outside Cartref, since there were no neighbouring houses. No, she would not know what kind to order. She'd go in person and ask advice in the shop.

A warm glow had spread throughout her. She settled into relaxed meditation, a velvet cushion behind her head. She gazed pleasurably through the window to the secure outlines of distant mountains. The rhythmic rain was soothing as harp strings plucking an old melody. She sat on and on, completely forgetful of the uncooked joint of lamb which she had noticed waiting ready in its pan on the kitchen table. With a third good measure of brandy, a decision swam up to her mind, from nowhere and nothing connected with the lamb.

She found herself at the telephone dialling Eirene's number. After a long ringing, Alcwyn's shouting voice could be heard beyond Eirene's 'Hello!' — '*Won't* take her dog for a walk. Raining'. Learning the caller's identity, Eirene said affably, 'You are coming to see me? This evening?' With no slurring of voice, Rhonwen said, 'Not this evening. I am phoning to say I am going to Torquay towards the end of this month, for a week, and I am inviting you to go with me.' There was a pause, which seemed long, then, with no hint of bewilderment, Eirene said, 'I can't afford it. No seaside holidays for me any more.'

'I told you I am inviting you. All expenses paid except pocket money. We will drive there . . . . The hotel room,' Rhonwen took inaccurate flight, 'was booked by Adda many weeks ago, a double room with twin beds and a bathroom. Hotel on the Front. Good food.'

Flurried, but plainly relieved by this astonishing gesture of armistice, Eirene stammered, 'Why, now . . . it is kind . . . Torquay . . . never been there.'

'We will go in memory of Adda. You will decide by tomorrow?' Rhonwen's voice had become peremptory, the voice of a woman with a firm hand for weaklings.

Eirene promised to decide by then and Rhonwen said no more. Back in the living room, looking at the carriage clock, she was surprised to find it was a quarter to three. But she returned to the chair and took another measure of brandy, the joint of lamb forgotten. It was five o'clock before she realized she was the worse for drink. She ate scrambled eggs, was in bed by eight and had a night of completely peaceful slumber.

Eirene telephoned the next morning. 'Look,' Rhonwen cut into a distracted inability to say 'yes' or 'no' about Torquay, 'I am just going into Melin to shop. You will give me a cup of tea at three o'clock?' Eirene consented readily.

First, there was a call at the optician in Melin. Dai Matthews was old established, of hazy qualifications (his father used to test eyes and sell glasses at the market stall on Thursdays) but capable of satisfying cash-down customers without fuss of appointment with a visiting oculist from the county hospital under the National Health regulations. 'I need glasses before I go to Torquay in a week or two,' Rhonwen said. 'Lately I've been seeing black blobs, rainbows and sheep that aren't there.' She sat before an illuminated chart of lettering, Matthews shone a torch into her eyes, she selected formidably thick black rims from specimens, and he promised, at a cost of thirty pounds, that the glasses would be ready in five days. He asked if she had been suffering from strain and tension lately.

'Strain and tension! I am the widow of the man who fell accidentally down Pen Mawr cliff. The inquest was in the paper.'

Next, she went to an electrician's shop and bought a dozen high-watt bulbs; Adda's skimping of light in the last few years was the main cause of her eye trouble, now manifesting itself in full. Next, she drove to the off-licence shop, situated well behind the Town Hall in a discreet turning; as with so many other taboos, annunciative pleasure in drink, especially by women, was still not the fashion even in a town the size of Melin. The shop was well stocked with rows of spirits and wines. A loud bell sounded as she pushed the door open, and soon a large, puffing man half-appeared from a trap-door in the floor. 'What do you want?' he demanded. Cantankerous offence might have been taken.

'You stock champagne?'

'For a wedding or drinking?'

'Drinking.'

Grudgingly, he emerged in full from the trap door, and said he had in stock three bottles of vintage champagne, dry. The price startled her. 'The wedding stuff is much cheaper,' he said. 'Plenty of *that* in stock. Orders only for the others. Sir Idwal Prys ordered these three by phone a day before he died, and his wife wouldn't take them. She said his senses had gone. No wonder she had to sell Careg Castle.'

The victualler eyed his new customer in an experienced way,

accepted her cheque, and told her that, yes, he could obtain most of the decent champagne at short notice. She put the wrapped bottles in the boot of her car, and drove to Melin's residential hotel.

With her three-course lunch she drank a half bottle of claret, lingered a long time over coffee and a comforting women's magazine in the oak-beamed lounge, and asked for a brandy. In its huge bubble glass the drink looked a thimbleful; she asked for another, and cigarettes and matches. A non-smoker, she inhaled in short, quick snatches. The chance that a Women's Guild member would look in was remote. Only English businessmen and a woman with an American accent were present. For half an hour she half-dozed in her corner. Her thoughts rose and sank. One of these persisted. With about forty-five thousand pounds behind her, counting the sale of Cartref, she could settle in a Torquay hotel for the rest of her life. It wouldn't be as drastic as disappearing to Australia, where in any case Marged did not seem to want her, though surely the country was big enough for one more woman.

She opened her eyes to find the lounge empty. The chairs had the peculiarly bereft look of hotel ones in which had sat too many anonymous strangers. A brass-faced grandfather clock ticked against a bulgy wall streaked with pitted oak. Did she hear a faint rustling or gnawing sound from the warped floorboards under her chair, where the carpet ended? Something was moving? She peered down. Nothing. The clock ticked peacefully, in the solid manner of its antique kind. She rose from the chair with an effort. She'd be late arriving at that woman's. Did it matter? Did anything matter? Oh, yes. A good standing in the eyes of everybody else mattered, and to maintain that position required contrivance. She must keep a watch on herself. A certain pattern had been woven over the years, and it couldn't, or mustn't, be torn to shreds. You could stain it, but the blot could be washed away by self-discipline, an aid to redemption. She drove rather erratically to the house in Camber Road, taking a wrong turning once, and at another corner in the main street a policeman eyed her progress with interest. She felt her liver was out of order and resolved to take a tumbler of purging saline when she returned to Cartref. Adda had always taken one on Mondays, starting his week in his usual ledger kind of way.

'Well, the rain has stopped at last,' Eirene greeted her at the door. 'Quite a wet weekend, wasn't it?' She might have been admitting an appreciated old friend.

She was not only dressed for the occasion in a pretty, freshly-cleaned frock, but her curly hair was newly arranged in a fashionable style, a faint scent wafting from it. Noticing Rhonwen's glance at the smart coiffure, in the living room, she confided, 'I went to Blondie and Blackie this morning. Time I had their hair-do, I thought.' That it was a compliment to the visitor was left implied. Only women of pocket-consequence patronized the recently opened salon launched by two adventurous young men, one blond, one raven, who had arrived from England, declaring themselves to be cousins, which some doubted, especially the nearby florist and ex-singer, Blodwen, who had remarked, '*I* can't afford to run a flashy sports car on flowers. Cousins, my eye!'

'It suits and alters you,' Rhonwen said formally. She had never been to the raffish Blondie and Blackie herself, and decision came to her now.

'The poet you met paid me something on account, and Alcwyn's father gave me rent for *two* weeks — he won something on betting.'

Over a quickly produced cup of tea, Rhonwen asked, offhand, 'You have decided about coming to Torquay?'.

The strange turnabout in tactics did not affect Eirene with such bewilderment as on the telephone. 'Is it because you want me to talk about Adda?' she asked. She'd had time to think.

Rhonwen laid down her cup. 'Yes and no. More no than yes. I want to get Adda out of my system. We used to go together to Torquay regularly — I expect you know that. You by my side there will help to change my memory of him. The same hotel, the same bedroom, and I expect Bessie, the chambermaid, is still on that floor.' Actually she hadn't yet telephoned the hotel to book the room.

It was all too much for Eirene to sort out. On the other hand, a week's holiday was offered her, and — who knew? — that demand for the house deeds might be set aside by this puzzling woman. 'You said you were poor,' she ventured, still uncertain.

'Poorer now Adda is gone,' Rhonwen corrected. 'Same as *you* are poorer now.'

'You said you wanted the house deeds.'

'We will leave that matter for the present.'

'You came here last Saturday to spy on me?'

'I was inquisitive,' Rhonwen admitted. 'What wife wouldn't be?'

'I was never a wife.'

'Why?'

'The young man I wanted years ago did not want me. He did me damage,' she added, a touch of moping in her reverie, 'I think, Dewi, the poet, would like to marry me. But I couldn't marry a man who's mad on writing poetry all his spare time, school teacher through he is.' She shook her head. 'Besides, he doesn't light a light inside me.'

'Adda did?'

'Not a full one, like a man should. But I liked his age, and he was dependable and funny.'

'Funny?'

'He wanted plain fun. A big schoolboy in that respect. He was fond of Alcwyn too. Bought him tins of watercolours and things.'

'It crossed my mind when I was here on Saturday that he was Alcwyn's father.'

'Well, he isn't. I would tell you if he was. No point in lying. I'm taking care of Alcwyn because his mother is off her head and I promised her. His father could look after a dog better.'

Rhonwen's nod of acceptance bore tribute. But she continued, obsession taking charge, 'Adda became miserly at home. In my car are a dozen electric bulbs. Hundred and fifty watts. He would only have sixty-watt bulbs in Cartref. He wanted to spend more on you. That is why we didn't go to Australia to see our daughter too.' Her face had tightened again, the obsession squeezing through.

'I didn't ask him for a penny!' Eirene showed a gleam of resentment. 'If he had gone to Australia he wouldn't see me for a long time, would he? Was that why he didn't go? Not to save money to spend on me.'

This little slap did not make Rhonwen flinch. She said, 'But he committed suicide'. There was no faltering; a simple fact was being stated.

A banging of the front door knocker concluded this somewhat repetitious colloquy, in which neither of the women seemed to have yielded an inch from her former position. 'It's Alcwyn home from school,' Eirene said, leaving to admit him.

Carrying a satchel, he came in at a run, yellow hair falling over his eyes, through which, drawing up, he eyed the visitor without greeting. 'I've got homework to do,' he announced. It could have been a hint for her to leave.

'You can do it upstairs after your tea.' Eirene went out to the kitchen.

Alcwyn flung his satchel on the large round table in the window bay, sat there and stared at Rhonwen. 'Can you make pancakes?'

'Nearly every woman can make pancakes. Can you do sums? Or are you a dunce?'

He drew his hair aside for a clearer scrutiny of her. 'I can pee higher than any boy in my class.'

'That won't help you to pass exams in arithmetic or anything else. Men think about getting on in the world by paying attention to arithmetic, proper language, history and the other subjects we've built your school for.' Her sententiousness was received without impatience, and Rhonwen smiled at him. 'If you will give me one of your pictures I will give you a tin of watercolours. My husband gave you some, didn't he?'

'Uncle Adda?' Such was the dilation of his eyes, that Alcwyn looked deeply suspicious. 'Auntie Eirene said he was dead.' At Rhonwen's nod, he asked, still wide-eyed, 'What was the matter with him?'

'Never mind about that now. Are you going to give me a picture?'

He jumped up, ran to the roll-top desk, took from one of its drawers a sketch book, and laid it on her lap. While he knelt beside her, she turned over the cartridge sheets, flatteringly pausing over a dozen paintings and crayon drawings of crooked houses behind gardens of blotchy flowers and bushes. Alcwyn, elbows on her thigh and hands pensively against his cheeks, gazed at his works in a non-opinionated silence, co-operative with her own. His pictures were an obedience to some impulse which, once satisfied, carried no responsive verdict in himself.

They were charming, in their primitive immediacy and uncalculated colours. Rhonwen held one page up, head aside, admiring a Noah's Ark kind of dwelling, complete with funnel-like chimney, built alongside a purple lake, and a flock of goose-type ochre birds flying, stridently alive, under a green sky. 'I like this one. I like them all.'

Deferential, he carefully tore the dozen used cartridge sheets from the top wire binding, laid them on her lap, and returned to the table with the book. 'I will make more for you this week,' he said. She was accepted, contact established. 'Where do you live?' Did he mean to deliver more to her in person? 'In Bedd. Above the village. My house is called Cartref.'

'Bedd?' He cogitated. 'It's where there's a stone that was a woman. Miss Pritchard told us about her in our Welsh history lesson.'

'It's a story people tell about the stone, not history — though a lot of history is just stories made up.' Rhonwen was enjoying herself; on the whole, she preferred little boys to girls, and the wish for one had always been a pang. 'What did the teacher say?'

He thought for a moment. 'A woman was very bad long ago and she was turned into a stone crossing a field in a thunderstorm. What did she do bad? Miss Pritchard didn't say. Alun Johns went on his bike to see the woman. He said she had a belly big enough to sit on, and there was a hole under it and a bird had built a nest there.'

'It all happened long before the Romans came,' Rhonwen said. 'They had stone tools then, and plenty of witches.' Eirene came in with a fresh pot of tea, fruit buns and buttered bread. 'Alcwyn is giving me these pictures, and I'm buying him a new box of colours.'

'Swopping,' he said, examining the tray set before him. 'Where's that jam you opened yesterday?'

Eirene sighed, went out and returned with a glass jar. 'Mrs Lewis next door gave me a pot of her new blackberry jam,' she told Rhonwen. 'She's always making jam, and keeps a pot of each fruit for me. I type letters for her sometimes in return. Do you bother to make jam?'

'I picked enough blackberries for ten pots of bramble jelly on the day Adda left me. A woman living here in Melin was picking in the same place as me.'

The room, bathed in the serene light of an autumnal afternoon, seemed rid of stress now, no curdling dispute evident in either Rhonwen or Eirene. While oblivious Alcwyn busily ate over in the window bay, Eirene lowered her voice to say, 'He can go for a week to my sister up in Pwll. I can't trust leaving him alone here with his father. He'd be half-starved.' She sighed again. 'I'm going to see his mother in Brynawel next Sunday. I never take Alcwyn there, and his father's only been once. Powell's run a special bus for Brynawel visitors on Sunday afternoons. She trims hats there a lot and I take her odds and ends for it. Once she tied velvet and ribbons on an old earthenware flowerpot and made another patient wear it for their walks in the gardens.' She glanced across the room at concentrated Alcwyn. 'There goes the last of that blackberry jam! He's got the appetite of a horse.'

'So you've decided to come to Torquay?' Rhonwen said, equally undertoned, two women talking of something enigmatical.

The drier, a Babylon warrior's helmet of shiny green substance, was removed from her head, and she scarcely recognised herself in the tall baroque mirror, with its couple of playful cupids topping a gilded frame between electric candles. First, there had been a face massage, then a shampoo. She had taken the young lady's advice about choice of style, and the resultant hair-do, with its fresh bronze glint, made her not only look but feel that many grey years had been sucked away into that magic helmet.

Eirene had gone for a walk on the Front, but was waiting for her on a gilded chair in the reception space. 'Expensive,' Rhonwen said, outside the velvet-looped windows.

'Worth every penny,' Eirene praised. 'Women though they are in there, it couldn't have been done better by Blondie and Blackie in Melin. I prefer men for hair myself. They take a true view of one.' It was she who had persuaded Rhonwen to venture inside the parlour on their third day in Torquay. 'There's a breeze on the Front, but the lotion will keep your waves in place. You smell nice.'

'I bought this for you there.' It was a handbag phial of scent. 'Too early to go back to the hotel. We'll have one of those Devonshire teas in a café I know. This way.'

Torquay was tranquil now, at season's end, its mildness relaxing one's nerves. Yet, in the pleasant café, Rhonwen found she could not eat the traditional scones piled with jam and clotted cream. Eirene could. Her own share consumed, she ventured into Rhonwen's.

'I ought to think of my figure,' she admitted. 'But there it is. I'm going to be fat later on, and it can't be helped.' She surveyed slim Rhonwen without envy.

This extraordinary treat of a week's holiday in a high-class seaside town was not to be allowed anything but pleasure. She would do her best to blot out grieving in her benefactress. 'Torquay,' she pursued, spreading raspberry jam and the dense cream on a split scone already buttered, 'is going to be good for my silly tear ducts, I'm sure. No trouble since we left Wales.'

'People come here after nervous breakdowns,' Rhonwen said vaguely. 'It used to be thought good for consumptives too . . . . Palm trees and cactuses.'

'And food . . . . That beautiful Devon beef we had at dinner last night . . . and the red wine you chose!'

'Adda used to order that wine. I don't know why I can't eat these scones. I had fancied a Devonshire tea.'

'Stomach too excited because you had your hair done. You look a different woman, Rhonwen. Your lovely ring too!'

Rhonwen had bought that morning a moonstone ring costing twenty-five pounds. Then there were the face massage and hair-do and purchase of the phial of scent. The day's extravagances, in a woman who had asserted a widow's reduced circumstances and demanded those house deeds, did not puzzle Eirene, ready to accept events as they came. In the long drive from Wales, the perverse oddity of the invitation to Torquay had not occupied her mind further. The weather was good, some of the English scenery almost the equal of Welsh. At the hotel on the Front a friendly woman receptionist had pretended to remember Rhonwen and commiserated with her on losing her husband. The same bedroom was given them, occupied by Rhonwen and Adda on a dozen visits. There were twin beds, a long window overlooking the bay, and a tiled bathroom, which Eirene much admired, her own at home giving her plumbing troubles and its water heated by a coughing geyser. There was nothing to criticise, so far.

They walked along the quiet Front to the hotel at its far reach. A crimson sunset promised, the easy sea had retreated, the breeze gone. A large gull, perched on a rail, eyed them sideways, predatory ruthlessness in its black, black dot. 'I don't like seagulls,' Eirene chattered, comfortable after her weighty tea. 'Nasty, greedy things that can never be tamed, I'm sure. Now, a canary . . . I took care of Dewi's canary once, when he went for a holiday. Sweet and trustful all day and never depressed. I had Dewi's tank of goldfish at the same time. You remember that poem he recited about goldfish, asking one of them to send him a telegram from its tail? Sometimes I wonder if he's all there, school-teacher though he is.'

'You never took him to bed?'

Eirene answered without surprise or hesitation. 'Only once. He was very upset when a special poem he sent to the National Eisteddfod competition was turned down. I thought it was the least thing I could do for his depression — and then it wasn't the bed, only the sofa.' She shook her head, the little heave of her bosom as dismissive. 'He didn't suit me, as I've mentioned to you before, haven't I? No feeling of a man leaping a stile. I think he imagines women so much in his poems that one in the actual body either daunts him or lets his fancy down.'

'You told me you thought he wanted to marry you.'

'On account of his living in a place like Melin. It's expected that a normal man in a normal job like teaching should marry. We don't treat poets as eccentrics, do we?'

Rhonwen gazed fixedly ahead through her heavily rimmed new glasses. Her coiffure still gave off a whiff of clove carnations. 'Mild here even with the sun going down,' she remarked.

'I noticed the menu card in the hall for dinner tonight. Roast duck with orange sauce. It's a pleasure to be away from one's stove and sink.' She patted Rhonwen's arm. 'Thanks to you.'

Rhonwen, after a moment's pause, replied, 'You were good to Adda.'

Eirene did not speak for a minute. The faint wash of the far receded sea, its long *ah, ah,* could be heard. In the gathering dusk the sunset became a smoky deep red. Gulls squawked brutally for a few seconds. 'I did my best,' Eirene murmured at length. Had Rhonwen's surprising tribute been an indication that the matter of house deeds would be abolished?'

'The poet might have sensed that you were only pitying him,' Rhonwen reverted to the failure of that compensatory act.

'Dewi should have taken it for what it was worth. I meant well.'

'Pity mustn't come into sex. Much better to go the whole hog and ask for a present.' Because they had reached the hotel entrance and, separately, entered the revolving door, the subject was cut off, but Eirene's eyes blinked several times as they crossed the hall to the left, as if a bout from her tear ducts threatened.

She enjoyed her roast duck, and Rhonwen, after gin and tonic in the bar downstairs, herself ate with seaside appetite now. A bottle of rosé wine shed a festive colour on their table. The dining room, open to non-residents, was nearly full. Except for Eirene, no one looked under fifty, their maturity reached comfortably with — at least outwardly, in a public dining room — little sign of pathological secrecies. In such a place of good edibles all seemed to be well with the nation, securities well earned, acrimony ironed out, decencies observed for an hour of four-course table soporifics. Service was excellent, its ceremoniousness much appreciated by Eirene, who noticed everything.

'There's a man sitting alone at the table behind you,' she whispered, 'and he's got his eye on us.' She meant on herself, since Rhonwen had her back to him. 'He was in the bar. You didn't notice him, but he kept peeping at us from above a newspaper.'

'Perhaps he thinks you're my daughter,' Rhonwen said drily.

'There's something about him . . . I know his type. They get it into their aura.' Her own underlid glances at him, over Rhonwen's shoulder, were more frequent than they should be. 'About fifty-five. A whole bottle of red wine to himself and has just taken a second helping of duck.' A mystical absorption seemed to descend on her. 'In business in London or a large city, and not worried about his job. I wouldn't be surprised that he's left his wife, or she's gone off with another man.'

Rhonwen paid little attention to these meanderings, accepting Eirene's roving interest as typical of her, and of holiday unimportance. 'If he's spending the night in the hotel I expect he'll follow you into the television room,' she remarked nonetheless.

After the meal she did not want to see the pair of television comedians who were Eirene's favourites, down in a dark basement room smelling of fungus, its chairs stiffly ranged together before the entertainment box. Glad of a respite from Eirene now, she went into the lounge, a becalmed place with an alcove fireplace, discreet standard lamps, leather armchairs and talkless people reading books or magazines. The occupants here were nearly always women, in pairs or severely alone. They wore finery for the evening; there were rays of colour, silks of brilliant magenta, silver, polka dots, glints of old gold jewellery, a flash or two of diamonds. Some were permanent residents, the fireside brigade, their chairs somehow proclaiming strict reservations; or there were spinsters and widows cast temporarily into this out-of-season haven, orphans from some inland region of monotony. They never went out in the evenings; horrors could lurk outside, there beyond the hotel's neutral windows, on the margin of a groaning sea.

She knew this bower of Torquay solitude, from the past, when Adda used to go into the bar where men outnumbered women. Taking a magazine from a table of them and sinking into a deep chair encouraging to well-fed snoozers, she turned a page occasionally. Could she retreat to this hotel in a disappearing flight from Bedd? Her home a chair like this, an anonymous table for eating in an adjoining room, and upstairs a bedroom with a view over a stretch of eternal water. She could spend every penny she had. Then what? *That* was a border at which her faculties halted. She closed her eyes, wishing she had not eaten so much, and ordered a second bottle of wine. The satisfaction of her hour at the beauty parlour had vanished, though the top of her skull still carried a trace of invigoration.

She dimly accepted that she had not only brought Eirene to Torquay to banish old memories but to lay a haunting . . . . Was there some other reason? She couldn't discover any. Certainly, since arrival her mind had not dwelt much on Adda, who had been so familiar with this town and hotel. Yes, his ghost seemed to have been laid. It was a wise move to bring Eirene . . . soon, like some others in the lounge, she dozed, woke, and was surprised to find it was half past ten. Most of the guests had drifted to bed. The next event would be a breakfast of haddock or kippers, bacon and egg, toast and marmalade, coffee with rich Devon milk. Then, full of a new sea-washed morning, gulls cawing on the Front railings, a stroll past the sunken flower-beds, tidily ranked with asters dewy from their own sleep.

She put her glasses in her handbag and took the lift to the second floor. That woman must still be goggling at television in the basement; if she had wanted the key to their room she would have had to come to the lounge. Advancing slowly along the rather ill-lit corridor, at its end an illuminated red sign indicating a fire escape, she heard a faint scratching noise from the flooring and looked down. A dark blob moved from the carpet, scurried along the few inches of bordering wood, and disappeared under a door. A beetle! But could beetles make a scratching noise? Jolted into full wakefulness by the tiny apparition, she stopped, put on her glasses, and peered closely at the door of number 8, beside which a pair of men's shoes lay, the only footwear in the corridor. Impossible for a beetle to have crawled under the door, which fitted tightly against the floor. Had she imagined both scratching and insect? Was there a rustling sound from inside the room, and a creaking? No, what was she doing standing outside this door?

A key was a fact, number 15 indicated plainly on a door, the ceiling light inside the room reassuring. She also switched on the table lamp between the twin beds, the covers of which had been turned back by Bessie, the old chambermaid Adda used to tease. She was already in bed, reading a paperback bought that morning, when Eirene came in. An uncharacteristic frown partially disrupted her face. In another type of person it could have boded a compulsive need of a quarrel.

'That man,' she said, kicking off her shoes, 'followed me down to the television room.'

Rhonwen returned to her book. 'What did you expect?'

'I don't expect to be followed about in a respectable hotel like a dog.'

'Is it in your aura?' Rhonwen asked in an offhand way, turning a page of the book. 'You mentioned in the dining room that he had one himself.'

Eirene's glance at her was offhand. 'Everyone has one. Some throw out an awful kind without telling its secret.' She removed a string of beads and spoke with irritable inconsequence. 'He's in dry rot and woodworm. Came down here to inspect some old property for his firm and make an estimate for treatment. Leaving tomorrow or the day after.'

Rhonwen put her book down. 'Did he get on your nerves?'

'He took me for granted,' Eirene said, beginning to undress. 'Said he'd noticed us walking in this corridor. He's in number 8. He asked me to go and sit there with him. Said he had a bottle of whisky and two glasses he always travels with . . . . I'm so weak,' she suddenly lamented. 'Weak. Born weak.'

Pausing to restrain herself, Rhonwen did not ask whether the invitation had actually been accepted and, if so, what had transpired. 'Quite close by,' she said, remembering the shoes outside number 8. Would a man put his shoes out for cleaning before his visitor had left? Of course, he might have changed into another pair before dinner.

Eirene's bra was stretched to breaking point. She said, again going off at a tangent, 'I didn't know you drank.'

'I'm on holiday.'

'Well, *I* am not a drinker. I don't keep any at home.'

Accusation sounded more definite. 'You've been making me drink in Torquay. Encouraging me.'

Was there an implication that another failing had followed logically? Rhonwen said, 'You've got a tongue that can say "yes" or "no", haven't you? You're not ten and still at elementary school.'

As she slipped off her briefs, Eirene was afflicted by an attack of her duct trouble. The tears poured. 'Where's that box of paper handkerchiefs?' she cried, half-blinded.

'The lower drawer of the dressing table.'

Eirene bent to pull the drawer open; it came out sideways, and stuck; muttering, she kicked it back and, bending again, opened it smoothly and rummaged, while the tears streamed. Rhonwen stared from the bed, eyes less milkily blue, a pin-point of fire within them. Eirene's apricot buttocks, a sepia birthmark on one, hypnotized her. She half-rose in the bed, and sank back, a wild impulse resisted. Her thoughts had strayed to the thin, tightly rolled umbrella, newly bought at Ann Jones's Boutique in Melin and, unneeded in Torquay as yet, hung by a tassel from a hook on the door. The twin mounds of placid flesh looked as soft as their owner's character. Had the cane of a feather brush brought weals to those sumptuous curves?

The unopened box of handkerchiefs, bought that morning at Smith's with the paperback, was found. 'I can't open it,' Eirene cried, eyes still suffused. Nude as her candour about that man, she approached between the beds, and Rhonwen's unsteady hand stripped away the perforated opening and took out handkerchiefs for the silly woman. Dabbing, Eirene exclaimed, 'And I was bragging that Torquay was curing me! Why didn't that man leave me alone? Are *they* the cause of my trouble?'

Turning her head away, Rhonwen said, 'Put your nightdress on.'

'I'm going to have a bath. I'll sleep better.'

'Hurry up then. I've been waiting to take my sleeping tablet.' Rhonwen picked up the book and, when Eirene returned from the bathroom smelling of sandalwood soap, her plumpish body gleaming from its laving, she was asked, 'Have you noticed beetles in this hotel?'

'Beetles? Not in a hotel of this class surely?' Eirene's nightdress, laid out on the bed by Bessie, had been bought for the trip. She ran her hand lovingly over the gossamer confection. 'True, we haven't seen the kitchens.'

'On my way in the corridor I thought I saw a beetle going under the door of number 8. There was a pair of shoes outside.'

Completely restored to equanimity, Eirene said, 'Did you have brandies or something in the lounge?' She switched off the ceiling light and climbed into bed. A note of earnestness came into her next utterance. 'Look, let's not drink anything at all tomorrow. It doesn't really agree with me.' She settled. Rhonwen's glass of water on the bedside table was full, her sleeping tablet not taken yet. 'Good beds these!' Eirene praised, the question of beetles abolished.

'How did Adda pass his time with you?'

'He often used to help me with my typing,' Eirene answered readily, 'especially when I had a lot of office overloads to do. He became quite fast. I remember he managed Dewi's Welsh poems better than I could. But he doted on business typing. It took him back to his Gas Board days.'

'You said he beat you.'

'*That* slipped out when I felt vexed with you. You upset me, that first time you called on me.' Eirene repeated her philosophic acceptance. 'That's how they are and we've got to put up with them.'

'You went into bed with him?'

'Good gracious, no. Undressing and getting into bed in the afternoons! . . . When Alcwyn arrived from school Adda would play dominoes with him or encourage him with that messy painting.'

'What about when there were school holidays?'

'Oh, I used to send Alcwyn up to his father's flat between three o'clock and four, and lock my front room door. Then I would call him down for his tea . . . . His father pays me a pound a week for looking after him. But it's a pleasure really.' Eirene yawned and nestled deeper into the pillows.

The guilelessness comforted Rhonwen. But the deep wound of treachery had yet to be healed.

'You never found Adda to be short-tempered or mean?'

Eirene focused more attentively on the unaccountable woman lying a yard distant. 'You want me to say something bad about him?' she asked at length.

'Yes.'

'Well, he never said anything bad about you,' Eirene supplied tentatively. She foraged, and only found, 'Men are apt to be like that. They're different from us. Less spite.' She searched again, and pursued, 'The only thing I found bad in him was the way his dentures clicked when we were . . . well, having love one way or another on that old-fashioned sofa in the corner beyond the fireplace and I opened my screen in full, though no one was likely to have reason to peer in at the bay window. His teeth would go *click, click, click.* Grinding them. It annoyed me. But it was just nerves bothering him, I expect.'

'Conscience worrying him.'

After a moment of ponderous thought, Eirene remarked, 'Conscience isn't born in them concerning sex. It's only been pushed a short way into them by a country's government and religion.'

'I never heard his dentures clicking.'

'People take their dentures out at night, don't they? For me, it was always afternoons.' Perhaps to placate Rhonwen, she found something else to criticize. 'He was too finicky. At every visit he would polish his shoes and brush his clothes and tweed hat thoroughly before leaving . . . . A man should have a bit of dirt about him. Not be like those women that are everlastingly cleaning their house, so that you don't want to sit down. There's a woman in my street who scrubs the floor of her coal-shed before a new load is delivered. Neurotic. Adda had a streak of it.'

'He exercised with dumb-bells and a skipping rope every day.'

'I gave him a skipping rope when he was on the Gas Board,' Eirene recalled. 'It had painted wood handles. I had kept it since my schooldays. He asked for it when he saw it in the lodgings I had then.'

Rhonwen lifted herself to take her sleeping tablet. In her face there was no hint of hostility. Eirene glanced at her, gave a sigh, and turned her head away, snuggling down into the good bed. Outside, the splashing of the incoming tide sounded more distinct when the bedside lamp was switched off, a melancholy impetus regular as the beat of a heart. Rhonwen was soon asleep, and dreams that night carried no threat. A trace of the day's events ran through them. She walked on the Front, wearing the hair-drying helmet. Then she was in a ship which had advertised a cruise up to Dartmouth, read on a kiosk-poster at the pier entrance; but instead a fellow-passenger told her it went non-stop to Australia. Then she was in Smith's shop looking at tin boxes of watercolours.

Bessie brought a tray of tea at a quarter to eight. 'Ladies, you are going to have another fine day,' she declared, swishing back the window curtains, a woman in her buxom sixties. She poured the first cups for the two. 'Just the day for a trip over Dartmoor. Bowden's run a good afternoon one in their coaches. Forty years I've worked here and hadn't been till last week, on my afternoon off, and at last Bowden's gave me a free trip for recommending them to so many. I wanted to see Princeton prison, but the duffers won't go near it.'

'I expect they think holiday people don't want to be reminded,' Eirene said.

'Brixton crab on the lunch menu today. They've just been delivered, a basketload with claws still moving about, ugh. I won't stay in the kitchen when the chef drops them into boiling water. I fancy they cry out like little babies, but chef says they're only breaking wind.'

'Enough to put one off crabs,' Eirene remarked when Bessie had gone. 'I like to see them properly dressed on a marble slab, same as the fishmonger in Melin does them. I remember giving one to Alcwyn and Adda for tea. It was Alcwyn's birthday. I made pancakes as well.' Pancakes on birthdays was a local custom

Rhonwen, sitting up in bed with cup in hand, said, 'I don't want to talk about Adda today.'

After a peep at her, Eirene nodded approval. 'That man in number 8 . . . he told me his wife had gone on a package tour to Istanbul with another woman. Said she couldn't stop going on tours, four or five times a year. He asked me where I lived and gave me the address of his firm, *and* his private one. He said there was sure to be a lot of dry-rot business for him in Wales.'

'Did you give him your address?'

'No. Not after he said he could motor anywhere to inspect and give estimates for treatment. I don't want a dry rot man turning up at my door or using me as a headquarters. He said something about giving me ten per cent commission on business obtained through me. He seemed to think the whole of Wales was tumbling down from dry rot and pests.' Eirene bounded out of bed, refreshed and abundant, 'Let's go over Dartmoor in a coach this afternoon.'

'It's only scenery, but it will be something to do and a rest from driving my car.' Accord, after the long unhaunted sleep, exuded from Rhonwen too.

'That man asked me who you were and I told him you were my aunt and had lost your husband lately and come here to try and forget.' And at breakfast downstairs, she observed, 'He must have gone'. The adjacent table was bare except for some token objects. 'That's a load off my back.'

After a filling lunch, but no alcoholic drink, they set out in a half-filled coach. It crawled up nude heights, and down to brown vales of dejected bracken, rocks, sprinting brooks and austere hamlets. Wild ponies were glimpsed, and grazing sheep. A stop was made at a refreshment shed beside a rampageous dash of water, and Eirene took another Devon treat of clotted cream, scones and jam — 'Winter is coming and I must build up,' she excused herself.

On the return journey, the humps of heathland and the twisted bushes began to withdraw into a dusky lack of assertion. Nobody walked even on these lesser heights. Rhonwen sat next to the window, and replete Eirene gazed half drowsily beside her, only speaking to ask to be reminded to get picture postcards off the next day, her second batch. Suddenly, Rhonwen whispered, 'Look!' Eirene peered. From a scrub of bushes on a near slope a sheep paused to gaze at the intrusive vehicle. It was full-size and, judging by its stance and aspect of belligerence, male.

'That sheep you mean?'

'It's a ram! Did you see his horns were red?' Already the coach had sped past a view of the beast.

Eirene, arrested by something in Rhonwen's voice, asked, 'Well, what about it?'

'Did you see his horns were red?'

'Red as blood. They belong to these savage parts, like those wild ponies we saw . . . unless,' Eirene pursued, 'a farmer paints their horns red so that he knows they're his property. Sheep in Wales have their coats branded with a black letter, don't they? What's the matter?'

'They were red. He stared at me.'

'Well, we're not in Africa with lions roaming about us . . . . Rhonwen, you're not well. And I think you are highly strung inside, but you put on a steady front nearly all the time.'

It could explain the drinking. A touch of protectiveness came into Eirene's manner. Total loss of Adda had unbalanced Rhonwen. The previous loss, of faithfulness as a husband, surely was of no weight in comparison — not nowadays. Eirene took the widow's arm, and they walked from the coach station to the hotel. On several occasions in Torquay she had noticed Rhonwen cast into a remote abstraction, as if gone far away into a secret core of her being where some terror lay dormant. This invitation to Torquay had still to be fathomed. Although the oddity of it troubled Eirene briefly, she sometimes wondered uneasily if Rhonwen would go the same way as Alcwyn's mother and end up in Brynawel, if only for temporary treatment.

The following days passed agreeably, with continuing fine weather. No thorny subject was raised. Even the dry rot and woodworm man was not mentioned. Sitting together one morning in the tranquil Abbey gardens, after visiting the jungle riot of exotic and ferocious plants in conservatories, Eirene, out of her own musing, ventured to say that she thought of increasing the rent of the flat occupied by Alcwyn's father. This oblique approach to the house deeds subject elicited no response from Rhonwen. Cast in one of her reveries, she murmured that she had thought of going to live in Australia, but now she might choose Torquay.

On the last day, after breakfast, she went down to the reception desk to pay the bill, and, her face gone pale despite the sea air tinting gained by the week, returned to their room, where Eirene was finishing her packing.

'I've seen him!'

'Seen who?' Eirene had a foot on the bulging suitcase lying on the floor; she had done a lot of shopping, including several presents. 'Not that dry rot man?' she exclaimed in panic, sitting plumb on the suitcase, effectively achieving closure of the locks.

'Adda.' Rhonwen's eyes were quite expressionless, fixing on nothing in the room 'He was standing on the steps of the front porch. I could see him plainly through those revolving glass doors while I waited by the desk for that coloured girl to make up my bill. It was *his* straight back, *his* lovat tweed jacket with the leather elbows, *his* green tweed hat. He stood looking across the road at the sea. I went out at once. But he had gone! Nobody walking the pavement, nobody crossing the road.'

'Rhonwen! What's the matter with you? You're spoiling your week, imagining things.'

'It was his ghost.'

'Come now. Put your new headscarf on.' Eirene snatched from the dressing table a peacock square of silk. 'Look how pretty it is!'

She arranged it on Rhonwen's head, tied it under the now compliant and even slightly quivering jaw. The arranging was almost a caress. 'You haven't put on any weight here, like me, though you said your nerves and sleeping were better, and no bad dreams. Come now. Seeing things! Ten o'clock in the morning's no time for that.' Her whole being exuded reliable health; she was a little sun of warm stamina flooding the shaken woman.

Bessie came to say goodbye, a porter arrived for the suitcases, and Rhonwen, more herself in the fuss of departure, went to fetch her car from the garage. All trace of the effect the apparition had caused vanished during her smooth driving to Bristol, where they were staying the night. Before they reached the city she suddenly abolished chatter about the scenery, the villages, small episodes in the past week. She said, 'Those house deeds I talked of, Eirene, and rents from you and Alcwyn's father . . . well, I will not press the matter any more.'

Eirene pondered to the extent of which she was capable. Rhonwen's right to the deeds and rent still remained a vague uncertainty in her mind, and, ever slothful in taking legal advice on any matter, especially such a delicate one as this, she had kept pushing it to the back of her mind. She asked now, with no show of accurate curiosity, 'What has made you decide?'

'When you told me you had not given your address to the dry rot man. If you had given it . . . well, I might have had a different opinion of you.'

Eirene said nothing more on the business, this further waywardness of the widow accepted without uneasy wonder. She realized, however, that she had been under assessment all the week. It seemed the main reason for the astonishing invitation to Torquay.

# Three

Despite the charitable week in Torquay, with its element of forgiveness, the haunting did not cease when she was back in Cartref, though at the seaside her dreams at least had been untroubled. Not that the ram returned every night at Cartref. Sometimes he did not appear as a visual presence at all, only as an invisible assertion lurking deep in the caverns of her mind, or as an odour pervading whatever meaningless dream she had. His visual presence could make surprising appearances which brought additional fear. Once she saw him coming down a store escalator behind a woman carrying a bulging paper satchel, and she fled in panic through a maze of ground floor departments; another night she saw him, front legs up on the counter, buying stamps from Miss Piper in Bedd post office. The escape to Torquay with Eirene was not, after all, an exorcism, and neither was the decision to drop the house deeds persecution. She continually postponed asking Dr Llewellyn to prescribe a different kind of sleeping tablet, convinced now that such would be ineffectual. She realized that an intricate problem of expiation must be worked out, or at least an obliteration achieved for which no sleeping tablets or medical tranquillisers were of use. Drink helped more, helping her to get through the day, a quiet if fleeting friend.

That she was a changed woman, if only in her smartened exterior, did not of course escape notice in Bedd. Mrs Pyle-Williams came to see her in Cartref, ostensibly to inquire why she still did not come to the Women's Guild meetings. And was it true that she had told the baker that she thought of settling in England?

'Yes. I fancy England. The English mind their own business.'

The president, divided between hostility to that nation and interest in acquiring Cartref as a speculation, remarked, 'I thought you said you were planning to go to your daughter in Canada'.

'Australia is where Marged lives. She doesn't want me.'

'How much would you ask for the house?'

'Forty thousand pounds.'

Mrs Pyle-Williams stared at her. Was the outrageous price a teasing snub? The owner seemed to be perfectly serious, and indeed looked as if she'd stick out for the last penny.

‘Now, Rhonwen, *cariad.* Fifteen thousand is the very most it would fetch. I ought to know about house prices in our countryside.’

‘There isn’t any dry rot or rising damp. But I’m troubled with blackbeetles.’

‘Blackbeetles?’ The visitor was alarmed, shifting her feet.

‘Can’t you smell them? I found one running from under my pillow one night, just as I was stepping into bed.’

‘Rhonwen, you must phone the deinfestation department in Melin Council Offices. They cleared out Mrs Catrin Pritchard’s mice in a day. Free of charge to ratepayers. Perhaps Cartref was built on an old rubbish dump.’

‘Adda used to say the land was supposed to be a burial place before Christianity came to Wales.’

Mrs Pyle-Williams, whose only mania was extreme nationalism, looked hard at Rhonwen. ‘How many have you seen?’

‘Dozens. They must have burrowed a new little tunnel from far down.’ A finger, wearing a decorative ring, pointed to the floor.

Mrs Pyle-Williams, uncertain of Rhonwen’s mood, changed the subject. ‘Now, are you wishing to continue as secretary and treasurer of the Guild?’

‘No; I can’t take interest in it any more.’

The president glanced at the stylized coiffure, the plucked eyebrows, the showy ring, a smart jacket gleaming metallic as steel. Had the well-off widow met a man in Torquay, an Englishman? ‘I can understand someone going to live in Australia,’ she declared, ‘but not England. Things have gone stale there. No wonder they want to take our houses and property here. It’s a bit like the invasions of olden days. We must keep them at bay, Rhonwen. If you put Cartref in the hands of an agent they might advertize it in English papers. Adda wouldn’t like an Englishman in Cartref, I’m sure. They steal our water, drowning whole valleys belonging to us, and form colonies of caravans.’ Automatically she had begun to seethe. ‘What do they think we are? Barbarians in Julius Caesar’s time? The Welsh were civilized here when Romans set lions to eat Christians, and an Englishman had never been heard of.’ In addition to her zeal for racial purity she had never really forgiven the English professor who snatched cheap, when her back was turned, the Bedd cottage she had wanted for a niece.

'If a Chinaman came offering me forty thousand for Cartref I would let him have it tomorrow.'

Mrs Pyle-Williams surveyed her again. Actually she was trying to fathom a mysterious change in her Women's Guild chief assistant. Gossip had begun in Bedd. Rhonwen had been seen by a Guild member coming out of the licensed victualler's in Melin carrying to her car an armful of bottles; and the husband of another, a birdwatcher with a camera, had trespassed into Cartref's large back garden and seen in a rubbish hollow dozens of empties, including champagne ones. So far there was no evidence of secret drinking — no puffy eyes, coarsened or inflamed cheeks, though her wandering attention and preposterous asking price for Cartref could mean an affected mind. Perhaps it was as well that Rhonwen did not remain treasurer of the Guild.

'A Chinaman? Or a black man, I suppose?'

'I tried putting down a disinfectant for the blackbeetles, along the wall-skirtings. But the powder wasn't any good. You would like a cup of tea?'

Mrs Pyle-Williams refused, and soon got up. The widow accompanied her to her car, drawn up before the wide-open garage doors, and plucked at her sleeve. 'Look in here,' Rhonwen pointed to a circular object on a shelf in the garage. 'Adda's ashes are in that. What do people do with them?'

'Terwyn Rowell J.P. keeps his wife's in an alabaster vase on a window-sill at the staircase turn in his house. New stained glass in the windows, a design of flowers. I don't like that canister, Rhonwen. Tin, is it? It looks cheap.'

'They charged me a pound for it. Called it a casket.'

The visitor made no comment on its position, there on a shelf among discarded junk from the house. 'People decide such matters by themselves,' she said, unusually non-opinionated, though she added, 'didn't Adda have a favourite tree or spot in the garden where you could bury them?'

'I must make up my mind.' Rhonwen's attention had wandered again.

'Yes, you must.' Mrs Pyle-Williams spoke with some emphasis. She meant it was time the widow pulled herself together generally, and not merely in hair-styles and new clothes. Seated in her car, she appraised, 'I like your hair done that way, Rhonwen. Do you go to Blondie and Blackie?' She couldn't relate the external changes to what appeared to be a mystery of reclusiveness. Yet Rhonwen's erratic mental coherence did not suggest listlessness or an old-fashioned season of widow's mourning. She avoided replying to the question about the hairdressers and beauticians, who, Englishmen on the make, were blacklisted by the president.

'Have you seen any red-horned rams around our parts?'

'I haven't noticed any. Why do you ask?'

'I thought I saw one nibbling at those bushes down there by the gate.'

Mrs Pyle-Williams turned her ignition key. 'Well, Rhonwen, I am pleased to see you *looking* so bright. Next Guild meeting is on the twenty-fifth. Change your mind and come.' Her investigation was inconclusive, and a trifle disturbing.

Rhonwen did not go to the meeting. Instead, she sent a letter formally tendering her resignation, but enclosing a cheque for the annual subscription, not due until January. A week later, Insurance Evans arrived on his new and powerful motorbike, which had ripped the peace outside. Goggled and with an orange head-structure, gauntlets up his arms, booted and black oilskinned of body — heavy November rain was falling — she did not at first recognise him at the door. Dusk had gathered. Misty gloom shrouded the garden trees, the flowerless chrysanthemum bushes fringing the porch lay sodden and beaten.

Had he too come spying? Or was the call only a sympathetic realization of her loneliness? He shed his dripping garments in the tile-floored kitchen and stood revealed as the same respectable guardian of people's sureties. The high boots off, she lent him a pair of Adda's carpet slippers, on of the few possessions she had forgotten to send to the Guild jumble sale. All day he had been on errands of assurance to remote farmsteads, bringing reminders of benefits accruing from death, comforting the agitated, protecting against loss from fire, damage from acts of God (with exceptions) or from the Devil's machinations. He said he had been to the end of the vale beyond Cartref and decided to give her a look up. His nose was bluish. In the living room she poured rum for him.

'Not too much, Rhonwen *fach*. Because of the bike. Stop! . . .

I'm glad I sold that tumbledown old car of mine.' The coal fire blazed. He praised the cheerful look of the room, and remarked, 'Strong lights here now'.

'The bulbs everywhere in the house are over double power than they were in Adda's time.'

'Will you have the house re-wired? I remember Adda telling me in the Bowling Club that he thought the old wiring was rotting and he must get it done.'

'It wasn't done. He wouldn't spend the money. Once, when I was ironing a shirt for him flames came out of the flex where it joined the iron inside a rubber band.'

'That wouldn't be caused by rotting wiring. Iron overheated and the rubber decayed, I expect.'

'I bought a new iron with my own money.' She sipped sherry meditatively, from a glass so small that gossip could have nothing derogatory to say.

'Rhonwen, I would like to advise you to increase your comprehensive house insurance. I am telling all my clients that. Prices of everything going up and up. Mrs Pyle-Williams increased hers the other week. That house near hers that caught fire made her think a lot.'

'She talks a lot too.'

'Your policy can be increased in a jiffy.'

Rhonwen shook her head. 'I might sell Cartref soon.'

'You've got ideas?' he asked carefully. 'Where to go, I mean.'

'America.'

'What, all alone, Rhonwen? Come now, you can't just walk into America. I thought you meant to go to your daughter in Australia.'

She looked about her. 'Can you smell blackbeetles? They've been worrying me.'

He treated this as of small account. 'A lot of old houses have those. It's the deathwatch beetles in the timbers that are bad. You can't see or smell them . . . . Scatter borax along your skirtings. Or dab paraffin along them.'

'There's rising damp in the house.'

'Now, Rhonwen. You mustn't say such things if you intend to sell. Cartref doesn't smell of anything except beeswax.' He gazed into his rum. 'What price were you thinking of?'

'Mrs Pyle-Williams wants to buy it.'

He played nervously with a button of his thick Welsh tweed jacket, in the breast pocket of which was clipped his neat row of five different coloured ballpens, as usual. Uncertainty of her was again manifest; he himself began to ramble. 'The Bowling Club isn't the same without Adda. Members ask me how you are doing.' He finished his rum. 'Thirty thousand is the value I would put on Cartref for insurance purposes, contents included of course. At present it's insured for fifteen thousand, if you remember. Too low.'

She suddenly lifted her head from deep reverie. 'Then increase the insurance to thirty.' She gazed listeningly at the uncurtained window. 'The rain beats and beats.' She finished her sherry and turned to look, indecisively, at the bottle on the sideboard. 'The ashes are in a tin on a shelf in the garage. Mrs Pyle-Williams said to me, "Put them in a vase on the window-sill inside the house".'

'Ashes?' Evans was defeated in finding suitable comment, and his murmured word could have referred to the grey deposit under the curved, well-burnished firegrate, dropped from the best Welsh steam coal. He gazed with pleasure at the lively short flames above, and, as is frequent with this brisk coal, one of the lumps let off a sharp little hiss, followed by a tiny explosion. 'Life in that coal!' he remarked, beaming. Naturally he was pleased that he had sold her a higher insurance premium.

'I wondered if Adda's ashes could be scattered on the lawn of the Bowling Club.'

Evans started. 'Rhonwen, the turf is kept in pure condition for playing on. It's smooth as a billiards table. We couldn't have grit on it.'

She rose to pour herself another sherry, so meagre that it still could not cause verification of gossip. He refused more rum, and, seated, she pointed at her coiffure. 'Those boys in Melin, Blondie and Blackie, must be making a fortune. They know how to compliment a woman — with their tongues as well as their clever hands.'

Was she drawing attention to the fact that she was not allowing herself to decline into self-neglect? Evans, still a little jumpy, took random advantage of her remark. 'Does your mind ever run on marrying again, Rhonwen?'

'You would like to marry me?'

Judging by her tone, it could have been a playful jest she had uttered. Across his face a momentary fear spread. But her question was also that of a woman with a freehold property, solid cash and an excellent reputation. Cornered, Evans nervously pulled down the ends of his inner cardigan and shrank a little, as if cold, his nose, now fire-reddened, twitching. 'Well, Rhonwen *fach* —' he began, and stopped. Red spread to his thick, middle-aged cheeks, like a young man's blush. 'You are making fun of me?' he managed to say.

'You mustn't tell them at the Bowling Club that I asked you.' She said drily. 'Men talk to each other worse than women, I'm sure.'

With an unexpected show of anger, he demanded, 'Now you are insulting me?'

'Go home and think.' She got up and put the cork in the bottle of rum, banging it tight with her fist. 'Let me know the extra amount I must pay on the house insurance.'

In the kitchen she helped him into his cumbersome motorbike gear, even placing the great orange crash-helmet on his head and fixing the cellophane goggle-visor. The glistening oilskin coat, high boots and headpiece made him look strange, ornamental, even enticing, and she stood gazing at him as if she would not scamper from a determined advance. He might sit at her supper table dressed like that. An iron pan of *cawl* stood odorous on the stove, chopped leeks and parsley, fresh from the back garden, on the scrubbed table, beside them a sharp knife and her shining pair of brass scales. The *cawl*, best neck of local lamb, root vegetables and onions in it, had needed three hours very slow cooking, and it was almost ready. Through pelting rain and December gloom he was going home to a lonely house, even though it was close to the Einion Arms, where he had his regular chair, its wood seat hollowed in the middle.

'You ought to keep a dog up here. Emrys James told me in the Bowling Club his spaniel has pupped. Pedigree ones.'

Her body gave a little shake. 'No dogs,' she said definitely. 'No cats either. There's no mice. Only beetles.'

She listened to the dwindling roar of the bike going through the lashing rain down to the village with its clusters of lighted windows, a roar plunging into a lake of silence. Half of the bottle of sherry remained; she finished it and, feeling more in charge of herself, all thought of the decked-up Evans gone, topped the *cawl* with mixed leek-rings and parsley for ten minutes' more simmering. She allowed herself a cigarette, and, beyond the flame of the match, did she see a black coin skimming across the floor? No. The strong overhead light would have made it plain. She took from a big earthenware jar a loaf of bread obtained that morning from Morys's bakery in Bedd, and sniffed its golden crust with appreciation.

She always enjoyed going to Morys's, and thought of it was companionable now. If she vanished into another country she would miss such establishments with ancestral life. People went behind Morys's home to a stone outhouse that had a massive coal-fed oven, the daily bread from which couldn't be equalled. On Christmas day Morys would rent the oven to families whose turkeys were too monumental for their own stoves. It was said that there would be as many as fifty fowls in the Victorian oven and quarrels were known to occur over identification after roasting; it was alleged that turkeys were switched in the marked baking pans during the random basting visits of owners. In one case, a vendetta had begun between two families which lasted for decades, and was not truly healed even when a son in one family married a daughter of the other. Elderly Morys's own son had refused to follow the gracious calling of his father and grandfather and was doing well in Cardiff as a radio technician.

The bread was delicious with the *cawl.* After supper she took generous nips of rum, a recent experiment with intoxicants, and watched television. The programme came from a Welsh station. She had taken a liking to pop singers, and tonight there was a young man on the rise to constellation status. His close-up face emitted stellar coruscations, mainly from his mouth of course, but a volcanic voice seemed to exude from his eyes, nostrils, pores, hair and belly. Even his brain-matter heaved with the primeval bawling, and as he pranced, every bone, muscle and tendon was unified with the song. He also sagged romantically into dreamy yearning. He was both the voice of a young nation rising mightily to anarchy and a lamenting retreat to the bosom of ancient enslavement. His performance over, he was a chubby, bottom-of-the-class boy with an impudent grin, the mighty python of his voice curled down into sleep.

Rum, she decided, helped her through nights without dreams that she could remember, except as a vague haunting. Rum agreed with her better than brandy or whisky; its warmth ran wide-spread in her body, possessive of its machinery and her mind. After another nip she lapsed into a semi-doze beside the dying fire, the television still on. Fleeting thoughts came of Insurance Evans in his apparitional panoply. Her eyelids rose and fell and, out of the television screen came a nasty smell, then a cluster of red antlers above a faint, triangular, slit-eyed face. They were not the pair of horns she had known. These antlers advanced to her and, even as they entangled her head and shoulders, imprisoning her inside the chair, they dissolved into polyp softness, octopus arms slithering down her body, her legs, and slumping lifeless on the floor. Her freed head jerked up, fully awake. She stared down, and there was nothing on the floor.

She could not go to bed. For some minutes she sat staring at the blank white screen of the television, then rose and switched the set off. Her steps were uncertain. Vaguely she made a decision not to drink rum again; it did not agree with her. She found herself in the kitchen. The brilliant ceiling lamp helped to clear her mind. The alarm clock on the dresser showed twelve-fifteen. She carefully spread newspaper on the table, fetched her bag of cloths and polish, and began to clean her pair of brass scales, which did not need it. As always, this was the one household task which could fully ease her, restore her, banish stress. By the time she went upstairs and took her sleeping tablet it was nearly two o'clock. She began to think more rationally, almost lucidly, of the ram. Had something gone wrong with her mind, gone out of control, and the creature slipped in there when she had no power over the everyday workings inside her head? She had blamed sleeping tablets which, even before Adda's death, always made her dream vividly. But she had not taken a tablet before sitting down to television. Had the ram become a fixture in her mind now, taken up abode there, a possession? Most often of course he was in abeyance, as if fast asleep, then emerged for some reason such as a reminder of his existence. There had been daytime occasions when she sensed rather than saw him waiting in the garden bushes. And there had been the time when she saw him on Dartmoor — but then surely he was a living fact outside herself, since Eirene had seen him too.

Before tearing it up, she re-read the last letter from Marged. It had been sent weeks before and remained unanswered —

*Dear Mam,*

*Your letter came saying Torquay did you good. I was surprised to hear you might sell Cartref. Joseph wondered if you might marry again, and he can't get over his surprise that my Daddy did not put me down for something in his will, with two children to bring up. Don't get married again, Mam. I could never do it.*

*I work hard in this house, it is too big, eight rooms, and costs too much, with the heavy mortgage. I often think of Wales and Cartref and still try hard to teach the parrot we bought Welsh words, especially Cartref, but so far it can't manage all of them. Linda May still eats too much and Joseph Small not enough. He keeps brighter than her though. Some day perhaps we all will visit you by air, if the money can be raised, which will surprise you.*

*Joseph wondered too if you had made a will yourself. Working in a bank, his mind runs on such things. He says, would you like his Weston-Super-Mare sister to stay with you. She was surprised to hear of Daddy's accident.*

*I think Joseph Small looks more like my Daddy than like his own father, and there's something about Linda May that makes me remember you, fat though she is. I have been having eczema on my leg, and Joseph get his chest and stomach trouble. I worry about him and feel he will not live to a full age. His work in the bank overtires him. But I would not marry again. When I try to teach our parrot Welsh Linda May does not understand that I want to be reminded of where I was brought up.*

*From your loving daughter, Marged.*

*P.S. Joseph said that if you are not satisfied with a solicitor about making your will, your bank will do it and they act quickly after a person has gone. He bothers and bothers about such things, I suppose it is not surprising. No more room on this page.*

The only deeply resented item in the letter was the suggested visit — a spying mission? — from her son-in-law's sister, a woman met at Marged's wedding and instantly disliked. That there would be neither emigration or a holiday trip to Australia was fully accepted now. A bond had been broken. Marged had already recognised her removal into a sphere where her mother did not belong; all that mattered now was the making of a will in her favour and in the traditional family way.

Winter had been prepared for as usual, stores of coal and kindling gathered in, thicker blankets on the bed, warmer cardigans brought out. An exceptional act — even a wild extravagance — was the purchase, by special arrangement with Ann Jones's Boutique, of a weasel coat trimmed with fox, priced at four hundred pounds, obtained from London on approval, and a discount of five per cent allowed on cash down. She wore it for the three days she spent at a Swansea hotel over Christmas, having refused Bedd invitations to eat the rejoicing meal there, including one from Mrs Pyle-Williams.

She could not bring herself to ask Eirene to visit her at Cartref, even accompanied by Alcwyn; somehow she knew it would not help in exorcism. On the telephone one January day she proposed taking Alcwyn to Swansea the following Saturday morning. Whether or not there was any connection with this kindness, the ram, after an absence of two or three weeks from her dreams, arrived that night, but came in a different guise, without any sense of threat or devilish possession of her. She dreamt that she was attending her Bedd chapel for an evening service, lamps alight. The building was half full of statuesque men and women who did not move or betray any sign of life. Down the right-hand aisle from the back trotted her ram. No one but herself took any notice of him, or he of them or of her. He mounted the steps of the pulpit, where the Reverend was giving his sermon from a speechless mouth. Then in the strange way of dreams, the Reverend was no longer in the pulpit. The ram stood in his place, erect on his hind legs, a forehoof turning over the pages of the Bible on the lectern, as if in search of a particular text. His hoof turned and turned, his loosely pouting lips close to the pages, red horns prominent in his bent head. She had a sense of herself laughing in an outburst of relief, a loud crash of laughter that was not noticed by the dormant congregation, only by the ram. He lifted his head and looked at her without censure. His eyes of clotted grey, with livid centre slots, established a benign awareness of her. She wakened still laughing, all unease gone, and lay for a while in the hinterland between dreams and reality. The sense of mirth ebbed away, and in the darkness of the room she uttered a little cry, like a wail, and felt the large double bed cold and empty about her. Disconnection from her former companion in it had suddenly become complete.

The trip to Swansea with Alcwyn gave her a pleasure she had not known for a long time. Oh, why had not a son like this been given her? He was all vitality, eager observation and greed. In a large store she bought him a warm anorak to replace a shabby jacket he was outgrowing. 'No, not that kind,' he told the salesman, 'I want a quilted one like Brinley Bowen's got in my class.' There was a choice of colours, and he asked Rhonwen if he could have two, but this was refused, and he decided, 'I want to wear the green one now.' In the Dragon Hotel he drew the waitress's attention to the jacket — 'My Auntie Rhonwen bought it for me,' he said, pointing at her across the table. 'Cost four pounds.' He chose soup and a leg of pork and told the waitress he did not like parsnips. 'Well, we don't serve parsnips,' she said. 'There's sprouts and roast potatoes with the pork.' He said he did not like sprouts either, found he could have peas, and said he preferred mashed potatoes to roast. When his plate of pork appeared he demanded, 'Where's the crackling? We always have it at home.' The waitress brought a saucer of burnt rind, he complained of the smallness of a dab of apple sauce on his plate, and the waitress, a trifle alarmed now, brought an extra amount. Rhonwen judged that his new anorak gave him this assurance. While he ate a fancy sundae, she asked, 'Did Eirene tell you to call me Auntie Rhonwen?'

'She said you were married to my Uncle Adda,' he recalled. 'Did you know my Mam?' When she shook her head, he said, 'Auntie Eirene won't tell me if she's coming back from the hospital or what's the matter with her.'

Outside, noticing a sweet-shop on the way to a cinema, he asked if he could have a box of liquorice all-sorts. In the cinema he fell asleep, delicately but audibly snoring, and, prodded awake, soon slept again during a famous action-packed spy thriller, suitable for children. It was dark when they set out for Melin, an hour's journey.

'You will teach me to drive, Auntie Rhonwen? Prys Richards in my class says he can drive his father's car and took his granny to the top of a mountain in it.'

'He was telling lies. You've got to be older to pass an exam for driving. I'll teach you to drive then.'

'Will you buy me a car?'

'They cost a lot, Alcwyn. Perhaps your father will buy you one.'

'He spends his money on horses and drink and women. Would you lend me the money and I'll pay you back every week when I'm in work?'

'We'll see,' she said absently, not really listening.

'I expect you've got plenty of money. How much do you put in the collection plate in your chapel?'

When they arrived at the Camber Road house, Eirene, her cheeks looking rounder with indignant flushing, quickly drew Rhonwen into the kitchen, shutting Alcwyn into the living room. 'I've given his father notice to leave my house,' she announced. 'He thought I had gone to visit my sister up Pwll way this afternoon, as I do every other Saturday, but instead I kept watch behind my front window curtains, and at three o'clock a girl of about twenty came through my gate and banged the door knocker. She left at five, trotting down my garden path, full of herself. I had heard him go to the porch door with her. I shot out of my front room and caught him going up the stairs. "Elider," I said, pointing a finger, "you'll leave my house in a month's time." He stood there on the stairs, hang-dog, like they do when they're caught at it. I told him I would keep and support Alcwyn, and he didn't argue, his chin down on his chest. A scamp. I threatened to tell his wife in Brynawel. Ever since Torquay I've had my suspicions it was going on behind my back. I won't have it. It will give my house a bad name.'

'You can't get rid of tenants from unfurnished flats, because of the Rent Acts,' Rhonwen reminded her. 'He might turn stubborn.'

'Rent Acts! If I get any such nonsense from him I'll blacken his name to mud in Melin. His poor wife shut away from the world in Brynawel! He'll go. He'll go. Let one of his easy women put him up. Long before we went to Torquay he tried his nonsense with me in the middle of one Saturday night. Knocked on my locked bedroom door. I shouted "Who's there?" and he bleated "Elider". Thinking there might be something the matter with Alcwyn, I opened the door, and there the scamp stood stark naked and in a disgusting state. Naturally I slammed the door in his face at once. Next day, he and Alcwyn came down as usual to share my Sunday joint, and nothing was said. But I would tell the Rent Acts people about him, and if he makes trouble about Alcwyn I'll tell the Town Hall he's not fit to bring up a child. His wife placed the boy in *my* care.'

Rhonwen had caught a glimpse of Elider only once, in the hall. A muscular bantam with almost bandy, powerful legs, nevertheless he pranced up the stairs in a twinkle-toe way, buttocks tightly fulsome in his jeans. He looked a stupidly affable man from whom no atmosphere of danger came. As long as his good wage as a crane driver was maintained, and there were pubs, friendly girls, six spoonfuls of sugar in his cup of tea, his expensive motorbike, and arguments over football, he asked no more of the world. It was unlikely he would make trouble over possession of his son. The thought that Alcwyn would be taken away had dismayed Rhonwen.

'I'm hungry! I want my supper,' Alcwyn had burst into the kitchen exclaiming with impatience.

'*Cariad, cariad,* you shall have two suppers if you like!' His emotional protectress knelt before him, caressing his long yellow hair, crooning with an extravagant amount of maternal affection. 'Oh you're a lucky boy to have Rhonwen buy you a jacket, aren't you! And I've got those lovely home-made faggots from the market for your supper. Look, Alcwyn, *cariad,* I've told your father to live somewhere else. Do you want to go with him?'

'No.' It was instant rejection.

'Now, *cariad,* tell me — have you seen him taking ladies upstairs on the Saturdays when I go to see my sister at Pwll?'

'He sends me down here to do my painting when they come.'

'It's a lovely jacket,' Eirene admired. 'I'll buy you a pair of trousers to go with it. Now, these ladies — you've actually seen them?'

'No. I've heard him letting them in and out, and when they speak on the stairs. Only one at a time, I think. He told me they came to play cards with him for money, gambling. He told me not to tell you and gave me more pocket money.'

'Ah!' Eirene rose from her knees. Judging by palpitations around her eye sockets, a burst of tear ducts was imminent. She snatched up a linen tea-cloth printed with a picture of the Tower of London, burying her drenched face in it. The attack soon passed. When she went with Rhonwen to the porch, she said, 'That scamp would take him from this house over my dead body. Alcwyn's poor mother helpless up in Brynawel asylum like so many driven there by the behaviour of these hairy apes. I'll tell him I'll bring up Alcwyn free of all charge to him. He'll go.'

Dusk closed in at four o'clock and, sensing snow, she went to the window and looked up at the rock-dark mountains afar. A movement close outside made her lower her gaze and she saw the ram come out of a clump of laurels down the reach of garden. Streaks of a stormy red sunset remained in louring clouds on the far rocks, and not only were the ram's horns as red but his eyes too. He stopped to look at the house, dipped his head as if about to charge, and then suddenly was no longer there. The telephone had rung. For a moment the wild thought struck her that the ram had set the bell ringing. It rang so seldom now.

It was only Mrs Pyle-Williams, making an apparently gossipy call. The president asked her if by any chance she could be persuaded to change her mind and resume duties with the Guild — so far, nobody wanted to assume the responsibilities of treasurer and secretary. Rhonwen remained firm, and Mrs Pyle-Williams asked if she had decided anything further about giving up Cartref. 'I will offer you Cartref if I go,' Rhonwen promised, not forgetting the help Mrs Pyle-Williams had rendered over the inquest on Adda. Another discussion on a price followed. Rhonwen mentioned that she had increased its insurance lately. Mrs Pyle-Williams said that a substantial house down by the river had been sold recently for eight thousand, and that included fishing rights for half a mile. Then she mentioned that she had seen a casket of gilded wood in Mocyn's antiques shop in Melin — 'just the thing for Adda's ashes, I thought, and asked the price. Only fourteen pounds. Old Italian, standing on claw feet. If I had a dear one's ashes to keep I would have bought it for myself. Go tomorrow and take a look at it.' Rhonwen thanked her and said she would be going to Blondie and Blackie the next day, her weekly trip.

She was unable to go to Melin. That night the snow began. It fell thickly for three days, with the same fixity of resolution as the district's rain. Bedd's entrances and exits were sealed off, as they had been in some other years. Nobody could reach Cartref. There was no post or milk. The main road below was impassable until the Council's new and expensive Canadian snow-plough could be freed from use on more important roads. But the telephone wires remained. A worried suitor could not have been more concerned than Insurance Evans. He offered to shovel a way to Cartref if she was in distress. She was not. She had plenty to eat. Her stock of drink was satisfactory too. People always prepared for these possible white burials. In December she had boiled and smoked a whole ham, from an eminent breed of local pigs; cold, or a thick slice placed in a soup made of dried peas, or chopped into rice and onions, it nourished her. She made bread, and there were tins of milk. No wind moaned and shrieked. Silence was lunar. When the snow ceased falling, thawing of its deposit was slow. The village lineaments below looked like an uncut wedding cake. Four quarrelsome robins came to the living room window-sill at regular times, ten a.m., two and five p.m. Rhonwen had cleared the snow from there and, at those fixed times, spread crumbs of biscuits and sponge cake. Their own inner clock at work, the robins would hop on to the sill and tap on the pane a few seconds before she stirred to the charity. She did not dislike the abeyance in this whole week of isolation. It seemed to bring an inkling of future peace, the normal transactions of life completed. Once or twice she amused herself playing with her brass scales, weighing almost everything in her crowded larder, jotting notes of exact measures of sugar, rice, dried fruits, flour and everything else, down to the half ounce. She thought of fetching Adda's ashes from the garage for weighing, but to get through the deep snow deterred her.

Was it the dead entombment that gave her dreamless sleep? Was the entombment a foretaste of that other oblivion? Even in the daytime she felt cancelled out, and the telephone ringing came from across huge oceans. Eirene rang and announced that Alcwyn's father had agreed to leave without his son, and this information animated her a little. Five days passed before the snow-plough reached Bedd from Melin, but no side roads were cleared, and Cartref remained cut off. Insurance Evans telephoned and repeated his offer to attempt a rescuing climb to her, and again she declined. She knew that his fidgety attentions would always — unless she herself suddenly made a galvanic move, as she had with Adda — remain in a procrastinating state. Like Mrs Pyle-Williams, he hankered after Cartref.

'No loose tiles in the blizzard?' he persisted.

'No.'

'Chimneys all right?'

'Yes.'

'House warm enough?'

'I've brought out my old paraffin heater for the hall and had three gallons of oil in stock.'

'Take care of old paraffin heaters,' he warned, the man of insurances. 'Wick is trimmed?'

She had taken some Scotch, and replied, 'I'm not a foolish virgin.'

'Seldom one of those anywhere now,' he wheezed in a strange chuckling way. 'Been to the Einion Arms today, but can't do much premium collecting yet. Time hangs heavy. Let me know when you want to hear a man in the house again. My motorbike is itching to be used and I've got a new oilskin coat.'

She almost wished he would storm the house nonetheless. She remembered again that a marriage to him could prove an insurance in other respects than those of his profession — he would bring solidity, and she'd rejoin the ranks of women married to pillars of the community. Glass in hand, she sat musing in fanciful abstractions. Then she remembered what Adda had been to her before he stopped treating her as not a woman, and before she had been stupid enough not to suspect that another woman had come into his life, younger, fresher and not scandalized by strange practices, accepting beatings with a cane philosophically.

In the silence of the white-buried house she felt her reason almost toppling. The old terrible feeling of impotence, when Adda rejected her as a woman, filled her again, brought a consciousness of dissociation from other beings. The sense of power that her violent act at Pen Mawr had restored to her was dwindled now. Even her daughter did not want her, except as a person who could make a will. She crossed restlessly to the window, nearly falling over a rumpled, now dusty Persian rug, and drew back a fold of the curtain. There were not even robins; it was not their hour. She saw a sculptured world of yellowish pallor. A full moon had risen over the distant mountains in a sky of hard purple. It flooded the valley with a dead radiance. Below lay a kingdom of the moon itself, bereft, with no savagery or danger in its deathly oblivion. The mountains were ramparts down which no ram could speed. Loneliness possessed every fibre of her being, a physical affliction, connection with other people had been utterly broken. It was then, at the window, that a decision stirred in the secret depths of her sub-conscious, remaining unformulated as yet.

After three more days the thaw was nearly complete. The river became a torrential muddle of grey slush. Pencader Powell, aged ninety-seven, had died two days before the snowstorm began and his body couldn't be taken to Melin crematorium on the appointed day. Neither could a coffin arrive, and his peculiar but strong and unmarried daughter, aged seventy-seven, had thought fit to drag her father, wrapped in an old, patched bedsheet, out on to the preservative snow behind their isolated dwelling; she had thought the blockage of roads would last for weeks. Many sheep on the uplands were found stiff as rock. Rhonwen heard such items in Bedd Post Office, from a member of the Women's Guild. She was on her way to Blondie and Blackie, the off-licence and other shops in Melin, and she wore the costly fur coat obtained in the boutique there. She intended calling on Eirene also, for a chat.

Lambs on the uplands were already a few weeks old, their daytime bleatings less modest in tone by the time breezes of early March blew and a few garden daffodils were in full trumpeting frill. Such a breeze, strong and dry, was running on the night Cartref burned down rapidly to the ground. Only the thick stone outer walls remained by the time two fire engines, one manned by Melin professionals, the other by Bedd amateurs, arrived on the gravelled driveway. Since there was no water pump to which they could have attached a hose, they could not have done much, except possibly rescue the resident of the house.

Distant flames had been noticed at half past ten, closing time in the Einion Arms. There was no reply when Ben Bowen, the pub landlord, telephoned Cartref; the line was dead. Such of Bedd's fire brigade as were available were assembled with some delay, five men, including Police Constable Vaughan, Insurance Evans and Ben Bowen, mounting a minor engine kept in a lean-to a little distance from the village centre. Meanwhile, sensible Mrs Ben Bowen telephoned Melin Fire Station, which dispatched its professional engine immediately. The pair of vehicles, one tardy and old-fashioned, the other speedily up to date, collided at a junction of lanes leading up to Cartref. Their bells had not been clanging in those uninhabited windings. The collision was not serious, nobody was hurt and the short delay of no consequence. Cartref was already a charred shell. Its floors and beams of dry old wood, crackling in fury, had wiped out the interior. There was an evil smell.

Rhonwen was found standing at a safe distance down the front lawn. She wore a nightdress under a fur coat, fancy bedroom slippers with white pom-poms, and she held an object in the crook of her left arm. The headlamps of the Melin fire engine were turned in her direction. Of course she was suffering from shock, though she was not distraught. She babbled coherently enough, looked benumbed by cold despite her fur coat, and repeated more than once that she couldn't reach the kitchen to bring out a pair of scales she greatly valued. Could it be found? Would brass melt? Then she remembered the scales had a wood base and, a single tear running down her cheek, she cried, 'Never mind, never mind. I've saved my life.' Without make-up, her lips pale and pinched, she looked older, her face also drawn in natural stress.

While the professionals circled the walls, peering into the lower windows, young Constable Vaughan asked her, in a considerably friendly and compassionate manner, 'How did it start?'

'I was sleeping and woke smelling something from downstairs.' She made an effort at further recall. 'I opened my bedroom door and felt heat coming up . . . smelt smoke.' There was another effort. 'I don't know what started it. But Adda used to say the electric wiring was old and wearing out, and he would not have high-watt bulbs in the house. The highest was sixty watts. After he died I had a hundred and fifty watt bulbs everywhere.'

Vaughan's face had the blankness of dubiety on hearing all this as a possible cause of the fire. Insurance Evans took her free arm by the elbow, as if she needed support. Peering at the gilded box in her other arm, he asked, 'What is that you are carrying, Rhonwen? Your jewellery?'

'Adda's ashes.'

Bedd's policeman himself looked impressed. Evans said, in a hushed tone, 'Let me take care of it, Rhonwen. You will be driven to the village in our engine.' She allowed Evans to take the decorative, papier maché casket from her. An emotional twitching of her cheekbones was noticed by both the men. That she had rescued her husband's ashes and not jewellery, silver or other valuables was a credit to move a man's heart.

Another credit to the principles of her sex was the regard for her comfort displayed by Mrs Pyle-Williams, although there was now no hope of acquiring Cartref, except its land and walls. Rhonwen had been accommodated that night in one of two Einion Arms bedrooms kept for stray travellers arriving to examine the prehistoric monoliths in the vicinity, especially the carved stone believed to commemorate a savage priestess. Dr Llewellyn gave her a strong sedative to replace her usual sleeping pill. The next morning Mrs Pyle-Williams borrowed from members of the Guild outer clothes, underwear and shoes of suitable size. Rhonwen had spent nine hours of unbroken slumber and ate a good breakfast. A stoicism in her was much admired, but she decided to spend the morning in bed. She refused to see a reporter from the Melin weekly paper, but saw P.C. Vaughan briefly. He was followed, expectedly, by Insurance Evans.

'The Company investigators and fire assessors will be down, Rhonwen. You think an electrical fault was to blame?'

'I *think*. The living room floor was ablaze when I ran downstairs and opened the door. There was a crackling noise and thick smoke. I ran back upstairs and when I came down in my fur coat and with Adda's ashes that I kept in my bedroom the hall was catching alight. I remembered to hold a wet towel to my mouth and nose. I jumped the two bottom stairs because I thought they were burning. The smoke half-blinded me. I banged my head against the front door but managed to open it and felt the wind on my face.'

'You left the front door open?'

She thought she must have; also the living room door; her senses had almost gone. She judged she remained on the front lawn for nearly an hour, unable to move, her bedroom slippers soaked with dew. 'I knew Cartref had no chance,' she concluded, 'and I had a strange feeling inside me.'

'What was that?'

'There was shock. But I had . . . oh, gladness!' She suddenly looked exalted even now. 'We get weighted down with possessions and if they are taken from us by an act of God, or something, you feel . . . oh, free, free! Moths corrupt possessions, blackbeetles from old burial grounds come up. I can begin all over again now.'

'I was right to advise you to increase your insurance,' Evans praised himself first. 'You're taking the best attitude, Rhonwen *fach*. Soon as they hear about a house gone on fire people ask 'Was it insured?' They don't think of the loss of things that no money can replace. Or of the shock. First you had the shock of losing Adda, and now this. But don't you worry about the money side. I will do my best to put matters through fast as it can be done.'

The insurance matter took several weeks to conclude. Evans spared her as much as he could from meetings with his firms' investigators. Long before the cheque was in her hand, she was a tenant of the upper floor in Eirene's house, new furniture of bad modern style around her, including a single-size divan, a change from the inherited four-poster of Cartref with its fussy curtains.

Of course she was obliged to visit Bedd now and again. Sympathy was rife to her in person, tribal loyalty very evident. In Bedd nobody ventured to mention the possibility of arson or of carelessness due to drunkenness; after all, nobody had actually seen Rhonwen drunk, there was only the cache of empty bottles in a big hollow among bushes in the back garden as evidence. Her character had always stood extremely high, by local standards, and dividend increment from her sterling past was to be expected in her misfortunes. Ranks closed against outsiders. In the cautious discussions of the fire there were short pauses, a hesitancy, and only roundabout opinion was expressed. But it was known that Mrs Pyle-Williams, at tea with a group of intimates, declared, 'Well, even if she put a match to the house, which I don't believe, the insurance money will be coming from England.'

What did not become understandable was her taking up residence, it seemed permanently, in half a house in a Melin street of modest consequence. With her means she could have bought or built herself a proud house in Bedd, where her ancestors had lived for centuries. Insurance Evans could not be drawn on the subject. Of course their friendship was known and even expected to reach the usual goal. He had handled the two visiting men from his Company with diligence and tact. The two took a great liking to the Einion Arms, a true country inn laden with unspoilt charm, and appreciated for a potent ale brewed by a small unambitious firm.

She found herself at the bar counter of the Trout Inn sharp at morning opening time and could not remember why she entered this shabby back-street pub. She ordered a large dry sherry, however. An hour later she bought some yards of thin, gay curtain material at a drapery store and, in the street with the parcel, could not relate to the identity of the woman who bought the material for no reason at all except an urge to spend money. The windows of her flat were already newly curtained.

The amounts spent at Blondie and Blackie's increased. The pair of pioneering young men had extended their premises and now, apart from the hairdressing, there was a salon for facial beauty treatment and even transformations of feet into more ornamental manifestations that is normal with the extremities. The foraging pair had experimented with importing a young lady going by the name of Yvette. She might have charmed a sitting hen off its nest, yet she was not a success with the Melin clients, who all preferred the magical fingers of either melodious-voiced Blondie or rasping Blackie. Their mud-packs earned special praise, and Blondie's plucking of superfluous hairs and styling of eyebrows had a butterfly's touch. Many redeemed women trod the Melin streets. Rhonwen was favoured with a weekly appointment. She was one of their best Pygmalion creations, plus her private good fortune in retaining her slim and straight figure despite all the home drinking. Going along a street, trimmed and smartly dressed, she looked self-contained in security, often smiling to herself in an interior kind of way.

Running into her as she emerged from the salons one afternoon, Mrs Pyle-Williams exclaimed, 'Rhonwen, *cariad*, you're a wonder. Ten years younger, if not twenty! I wish my principles allowed me to support those two foreigners. But cheating nature can't be cheap, I'm sure.'

'I deserve a few pleasures after the blows I've had,' Rhonwen reminded her. 'I'm trying to change my luck.'

'Did you get the full insurance valuation of Cartref?'

'A bit less. You're looking at my new brooch. I bought it at Isaac's last week. I wouldn't like to say how much it cost.'

'You must mention it in your new insurance on where you live now. Why don't you come and give an afternoon talk to the Guild? Something about beginning a new life at your age, especially what it's done to your mind.' A hint of shrewd suspicion lay in the tone.

Rhonwen shook her head. 'I couldn't make it a cheerful talk . . . . I never thanked you for letting me know where to find that beautiful casket for Adda's ashes. I keep it on my new sideboard. You must come to my flat to tea soon. I will phone you.'

Evans had visited her in Camber Road and seen her tasteless conventional furniture, such as a person uninterested in the pleasures of the eye would buy at a local shop. 'My friend downstairs earns her living at typing,' Rhonwen explained the sounds heard in the hall, 'and she looks after a little boy whose mother was taken to

Brynawel. She won't claim his support from his good-for-nothing father.'

On a second visit, Alcwyn himself opened the front porch door to Evans, who hadn't come on his motorbike, and told the caller, 'Eirene says we don't want any ice-cream today.' A van with a musical chime happened to be drawn up across the road. The caller's identity disclosed, Alcwyn said, 'Oh you want Auntie Rhonwen? Are you the one courting her?' Advancing behind him, Eirene's face bore a guilty flush. 'You are Mr Evans, come about Rhonwen's insurance? She's at home. Please go upstairs and open the door by the brass knob you'll see on it.' There was an odour of boiling cauliflower in the hall.

He found Rhonwen reclining in a plumply bulging settee, glass of scotch and water in hand. A large coloured television set was illustrating the beauty of a South Seas Island. 'I've brought your new insurance policy,' Evans said, settling into a matching chair of the three-piece suite, after pouring himself a scotch. She asked him to switch off the television and nestled deeper into the settee, placing bright scatter-cushions behind her head.

'Not much commission for you on this new policy. Cartref was a palace in comparison.' She considered his bluff, trusty, weather-used face with detachment and laid aside the long envelope containing the policy for insurance of the flat's contents only. 'When's your birthday, Dan?' It was the first time she had ever spoken his Christian name to him.

'I don't keep them. They're best forgotten.'

She did not ask him what he would like as a recognition of his zeal for her. The valuable gold watch he had already received in memory of Adda no longer counted. It wouldn't do to offer him money. She lay musing, and inquired, 'Your motorbike keeping well, is it?'

'I've only had it a few months.'

'Ever been on a sea cruise?'

'I don't like the sea. I went once on a steamer from Cardiff to Ilfracombe, and that was enough.' Disregarding her apparent beating about the bush, he asked, in a professional manner, 'You are paying rent to the lady owning this house? You said I'm to insure only the contents of this flat, including your clothes and the jewellery you've been buying.'

'No rent. Eirene worked with Adda on the Gas Board for a while, and she wants my company in the house. I shall be remembering her in a new will I want to make.' Actually a rent of four pounds was paid weekly in cash, left under a mantelpiece vase downstairs every Saturday, an arrangement which, in some feminine irrational way, relieved Eirene from the necessity of declaring it as income for taxation, as it had with Alcwyn's father. Private money passed between friends was no business of a greedy nation.

Over his refilled glass, and Rhonwen's own, Evans became, as at Cartref, beset by indecisions and doubts that he could not pin down. After a moment he asked, 'You have heard from Marged lately?'

'Marged?' She looked vague. She had taken from her crocodile-skin handbag a mirror and vermilion lipstick, and ran another layer on the enlarged aperture of the small mouth that was born to purse easily. 'Marged?'

'Your daughter in Australia.'

She shut the bag with a very sharp *click*. 'Marged shows no sign of wanting me in Australia. I can't remember whose turn it is to write.'

'You are going to have the telephone installed?'

'No. Eirene's got one downstairs. I mustn't be extravagant now I'm a widow and Adda's pension is no more.'

Evans smiled to himself, familiar with people's little humbugs in the matter of economics, mere expression of which was a nourishment. At a rough guess he estimated her cash capital at seventy thousand pounds now that the Cartref insurance money was paid. He looked at her smart frock, jade earrings, burnished face and coiffure. Even the little whiff of perfume coming from her somehow proclaimed lack of anxiety. He said, 'If anybody in Melin wants you to put capital into a business, ask me first. I hear a lot about commercial affairs in the Bowling Club and the Einion Arms. Mabon Telfer's widow took partnership in a boarding house up on the way to Pen Mawr and hasn't had a penny back. A few August tourists, then nobody. All she's got is this splendid scenery and it's driving her mad.'

‘Why don’t you get married again, Dan?’ she asked, more aware of the solid fact of his presence, with its exuding of constancy and the loyalty of old communities well-rooted as the oaks of the lanes.

‘You went into that subject before.’ Was she making fun of him again? No. He looked at her thoughtfully, unease lessening. She was one of the quiet little women, never thrusting herself forward, not bossy, not banner-carrying like Mrs Pyle-Williams. That she had taken to the bottle evoked little hostile criticism in him or in others. Residual virtue from generations of chapel-going ancestors could stand up to a failing or two. She might yet make a good wife for an insurance agent with a reputation to match hers.

‘I had thought you might like to marry me,’ she said, holding out her crystal goblet for him to pour yet another measure.

‘You are teasing me?’ The thin stream of golden liquid was not quite steady as he poured. He took a shorter measure for himself and sat on the edge of his chair, his body slightly wobbling as if from anger. He remembered the boy’s question at the front door — ‘Are you the one courting her?’ What had Rhonwen, perhaps in her cups, said about him to these persons downstairs? Laughing at him?

She ran off into another subject. ‘Isn’t that box on the sideboard pretty?’ She pointed at the Italianate claw-footed casket on the mass-produced sideboard. The gilded and painted box was flanked by a pair of two-branched, silver-plated candlesticks, sham Georgian and without candles. ‘Adda’s ashes are in it.’ That she had handed the casket to him on the Cartref lawn on the night of the fire evidently was forgotten.

Evans sat back more calmly, relieved that she had apparently by-passed the suggestion of marriage. Her oddity in keeping Adda’s ashes in the living room was perhaps a token of a wife’s true fidelity, like the rescuing of the ashes when Cartref went on fire. He couldn’t imagine a husband going so far. ‘Adda’s name is often brought up by members of the Bowling Club,’ he himself rambled, making conversation.

‘Would they like his ashes to be scattered on the bowling lawn?’

He stared at her almost in panic. Was she drunk? Her voice wasn’t slurred, but a rosy tint on her dapper nose and a certain gleam in her pale blue eyes were unusual. ‘Rhonwen,’ he replied, solemnly, 'You mentioned that before too . . . . It wouldn't be suitable. Members wouldn't like their bowls to roll over his ashes. And the turf is kept as smooth as satin.' He began to look annoyed. Indecision had increased. There she was, reclining invitingly on the settee, a woman with a fortune which she might, in her cups or a dotty spasm, throw away by marrying some calculating Melin ruffian alert to her foolish weakness and who might encourage her to drink herself to an early death. Why, why couldn't he take the plunge?

'When one is used to the warmth of a man lying beside one for over thirty years, nights without it can be bad for the nerves.' After this, she patted her hand over her mouth. 'Scotch makes me yawn. What did you do with your wife's ashes?'

'She was buried, not cremated.'

'They're like a body. You can't just put a husband's ashes into the rubbish bin for Wednesday collection.'

'Rhonwen *fach*; you're drunk!' he said at last.

She nodded her head slowly, up and down, up and down. Yet in her preoccupation she seemed not to have heard the accusation. She said, 'I pushed Adda over Pen Mawr'.

It was to be expected that Evans was struck dumb. A blankness preceded a twitching of his face. He blinked, he stared at her. His gaze was not returned. The forefinger of her left hand, its nail lacquered pink, scratched lightly at the pointed chin which at certain times could look formidably enlarged into grimness. She seemed about to utter another revelation, but it did not come. A sigh came instead. She settled deeper into the green, orange and black scatter-cushions, like a woman given much-needed relief by confession.

Evans exclaimed, indignantly, 'Rhonwen, you must stop drinking. It can lead to brain damage.'

'I didn't actually *push* Adda. I was behind him when he stood on the edge of Pen Mawr doing his deep-breathing exercises. I crawled from where I was unpacking our picnic basket and hooked the handle of my father's walking stick around his ankle. I *pulled*.'

Evans's further exclamations were immediate. 'You're not well, Rhonwen. You've had a breakdown. Cartref going on fire was too much for you — it sent you over the top.' In addition to a normal reaction of disbelief he appeared to be shaken to the depths by inexperience in dealing with an intoxicated woman.

At the reference to Cartref a faint smile hovered on her vermilion lips. But she made no reference to the fire, considerate of the peace of mind and integrity of her insurance agent, who was so protective of her. She went on, 'After Adda died he became a red-horned ram and haunted me in Cartref.' She added, 'Until Cartref was no more and I came to live here. I've never seen him since coming to live in this house.'

'Your mind is disturbed, Rhonwen!' Evans was floundering helplessly now. 'Strain and depression are telling on you more now. Delayed action of shock. Nobody in Bedd would believe that you sent Adda over Pen Mawr. Why, it's been common knowledge for years what a good wife you are. Adda kept boasting about it in the Bowling Club bar when the subject of marriage came up. Quite a legend you were!'

'I was obedient,' she admitted, 'outwardly.'

'Treasurer of the Women's Guild for years too,' he continued to protest. 'You'll be saying next that you cooked the accounts.' He controlled his agitation. 'You've registered with a doctor in Melin? Or are you still with Euros Llewellyn in Bedd?'

Her faculties seemed to be perfectly normal as she replied, 'Oh, I haven't bothered to change doctors yet. All I need is renewal of prescription for sleeping tablets, and I can do that by post. There's nothing else the matter with me.'

Wind regained after the outrage to his common sense, he asked, 'This lady friend downstairs — you confide in her?'

'Eirene? I took her to Torquay with me last October, and we shared the hotel room Adda and I used to sleep in. She's never been married. We share a Sunday joint, beef or lamb, but otherwise there's nothing between us.' His meaning seemed not to have really penetrated her mind, and her reply now puzzled him.

'Now, Rhonwen, you must take medical advice,' he said, briskness rescuing him further.

'For what?'

'Nervous strain. It can bring delusions. Family doctors send cases to psychiatrists now. One of my clients told me his sister was sent to Brynawel for out-patient treatment. Acute depression. You can go as a voluntary in-patient if you're advanced in delusions.' He hurried on, 'Just tell your doctor you've been depressed and imagined things and —' he hesitated.

'Taken to drink? Well, I have and I haven't. I can go a whole day without a drop . . . . Come in.' The door had been tapped. Alcwyn entered.

'Eirene asks what is the meaning and right way to spell these words.' Kneeling on the settee beside Rhonwen's thighs, Alcwyn gave her a slip of paper. 'She said the insurance man might know if you don't.'

While she studied the paper, putting on her diamanté-rimmed glasses from her handbag, Alcwyn nestled against her bosom, eyes pondering on Evans. She said, 'Dan, my friend wants to know the correct spelling of "*rhyfeddol*" and "*annymunol*". I expect she's too busy to come up herself. She's typing a new poem by Dewi Dowdall-Jones, who lives in this street and drops in several pages most mornings on his way to teach in the comprehensive school. His handwriting is bad . . . Doesn't "*rhyfeddol*" mean "flabbergasted"?'

'No. It means "wonderful".'

'Alcwyn, find the ballpen in my bag.' He rummaged interestedly in the bag and, while she jotted down Evans's translation, opened a powder-compact, sniffed enjoyably, and dabbed the pad on his nose. 'Two d's together in "*rhyfeddol*"?' Evans said there were two. She spelt out the word '*annymunol*'.

'Correct. It means "unpleasant".'

'If I were Eirene, poor woman, I would say "No" to typing Dewi's poems in Welsh. He's always sending them to the National Eisteddfod competition and failing.'

Alcwyn's head returned to her bosom, a finger playing with an ornate brooch on her shoulder; he said that her front smelt nice. Evans was flooded with relief. The pleasing domestic spectacle of an ordinary small boy huddled against Rhonwen swept away the last of his dismay and confusion. He would not have expected humour, plain, malicious or bizarre, from Rhonwen, but her remarkable, though casual, revelation or confession of minutes ago seemed to be of that ilk — inflamed by whisky, no doubt. The suspicion that she had been making fun of him returned; her suggestion of marriage surely derived from the same alcoholic source. Had the interruption by this boy been pre-arranged by the two women? He sat in aggrieved pondering. Women were not be fathomed in depth. All-male huddles such as the Bowling Club were wholesome and wise, helping to keep a sane balance in life. If Rhonwen had been a somewhat younger woman he would have suspected that she was undergoing the full disruptions of menopause. He gazed again at the spectacle on the settee, the boy so sure of her affection, she so judicious in her demonstration of it. He even began to doubt that she had really spoken the terrible self-accusation; or he had misunderstood its wording. Perhaps a momentary delusion had afflicted *him*, after three whiskies.

She was replying to Alcwyn's questions about King Arthur's Court. Downstairs he was making watercolours of its characters; his school class had already been taken on a day's coach trip to Caerleon. As soon as he had gone, with the slip of papers, Evans prepared to leave too. For some minutes, finding it difficult to make a decisive exit, he spoke of a few insignificant happenings in Bedd. She did not refer again to her revelation, and he became more convinced that a strange aberration had afflicted her. Best to forget it all.

It was no affliction confined to Evans's visit. Scarcely a week had passed before, in Mrs Pyle-Williams's white-panelled drawing-room at Plas Clynnog, the same revelation drew to what sounded its conclusion — 'I did it in a temper. He got on my nerves for years with his meanness, and he turned his back on me at nights. It made me mad.' Half-vaguely, she proceeded, 'There were other things than those. They wore me down.'

Mrs Pyle-Williams looked at her afternoon visitor with some astonishment, through which a reserved kind of concern flitted, though basically her demeanour remained composed. 'Now, Rhonwen,' she commented, allowing herself more than a hint of scolding, 'the inquest verdict was accidental death, and even if he committed suicide, as some might think, a verdict is a verdict. If my memory is clear, you gave all the necessary information in the investigation beforehand. So there was no need for the coroner to question you. True, I had helped by speaking up for your character to his wife, Babs. If there were any suspicious circumstances the inquest would have been adjourned . . . and,' she proceeded with emphasis, a note of exasperation darting out of it, 'there would not have been an order granted for cremation immediately after the inquest.'

'I pushed him over Pen Mawr.' Rhonwen's quietude of face and utterance did not yield any hint of her reason or motive in making her disclosure, but in her very blankness and lack of hysteria there might be a clue.

'You said just now that you *pulled* him with your father's walking stick.' There was a touch of triumph in catching Rhonwen out in a detail. 'Wouldn't he have fallen backwards to the ground?'

'No, forward. I was lying behind him on the grass, flat on my stomach. Pushed or pulled, what does in matter? He went over the cliff.' Rhonwen kept silent during the minute of absorbent scrutiny she was given, then continued in the same dispassionate way, 'I set fire to Cartref too. It was easy. The old floorboards were warped and dry as a bone. I turned back a carpet in the living room and soaked a few boards with paraffin.'

Mrs Pyle-Williams stroked a silken-haired Pekinese lying somnolent in her lap. The simple action soothed her. Compassion came to her rescue too. That the normal gossip about the Cartref fire seemed to be verified as truth did not deter her from rejecting it; as gossip it was harmless and even a joke, but as fact it was stated by a woman who, a few minutes after confessing to murder, was clearly in a disordered state of mind. 'You're upset, Rhonwen,' she remarked mildly. 'Everything has been too much for you.' She pointed out, 'Insurance men are not deceived, as a rule. Dan Evans is not a fool, and two men from his company came here to nose around. You dreamt it all, *cariad.*'

'It was a red-horned ram I dreamt about. He made me decide to burn the house down. Haunting me. He was Adda.'

Mrs Pyle-Williams was the only Bedd resident possessing a living-in housekeeper, aided by a daily maid. They could be heard disputing in shrill everyday Welsh in the kitchen, and sound of their antique, wholesome syllables brought succour to their employer, like her stroking of the lap-warming Peke. 'Have you told Dan Evans you set fire to Cartref?' she asked, detachedly. Knowing of the see-saw friendship between the two, the question was permissible, here in a secluded room.

'No, I only told him about getting rid of Adda over Pen Mawr. I didn't want his company to think him careless, if the business reached their ears in London. Dan is a good man. He looks after me. He had advised me to increase the sum Cartref was insured for.'

'Everybody sensible does that nowadays.'

'It wasn't for money I set fire to Cartref. The red-horned ram kept coming there at nights to torment me.'

The expression of a person reaching a finally positive opinion came to Mrs Pyle-Williams's face, a familiar resting place of it. She ceased stroking the dog. 'Look, *cariad*, I must speak. We are Bedd women together in private here, and we are women of the world. You served the Guild well and faithfully for years. The Committee has thought of giving you a supper in the Memorial Hall and making a presentation of a cut-glass bowl or something, when you had settled down after all your bad luck. Now I will speak plainly. It is said you drink a lot.' She stopped for a possible comment, which came meekly enough, Rhonwen's pale blue eyes without a gleam of repudiation or anger.

'Do all drinkers do what I did?'

'Their minds can get blown about in one way or another. Before you started drinking you were not the type to imagine what you say you did. I would say you should go to Brynawel for advice about treatment. It's an up-to-date place for mental cases now. I know a J.P.'s wife in Melin who is on the board of governors. Would you like me to speak to her for you? I remember her talking of electro-shock treatment in Brynawel. It does wonders, she said, and they're very busy with it.'

Rhonwen shook her head. 'I'm not a liar,' she said.

'Rhonwen, this is not fair to all the people who helped you, including the police. It makes us all look foolish. Rhonwen, I never thought you were a trouble-making woman.'

Rhonwen took up her handbag from the snow-white carpet. 'I've spoken the truth.'

'Now you are here in Bedd why don't you call on Dr Llewellyn?' No attempt was made to detain the visitor.

'Yes. I'm going to see Vaughan the policeman first.'

She left without further discussion. Within twenty minutes, after a pause for thought in a tranquil lane, she stopped her car before a detached modern house in Bedd's straggling main street, a little way beyond the shopping part. A blue glass lamp marked *Police* hung above the porch. Vaughan opened the door to her ring, hands wet, striped braces holding up his thick, hard-wearing uniform trousers.

He had not seen Rhonwen since the Cartref fire business when a meagre amount of jottings into his notebook was necessary. 'Well now, a pleasure!' he greeted her, showing no surprise, and beaming in a quick, ready way. 'Come in, come in. Hannah has gone to Melin, and I'm looking after the babies. I'm not on points duty until midnight.' He was on top of the world. He was already a doting father of twins, and Hannah was pregnant again. After his gruelling experience with his first wife, the London trollop whom he married when he was a Welsh Guards corporal, all was successful now. Bedd itself gave him almost no trouble, a natural village where people knew when and how to close their mouths and also how to exercise their own system of punishments for misdoings.

'I've come to see you, not Hannah.'

'I'm washing the twins' nappies in the kitchen.' Their bawls, piercing with inherited health, came from a back room. 'You want me to put on my tunic? Business, is there?' A room on the left of the hallway was kept for that.

'Yes. Let's go to the kitchen. I want to see the twins.'

They were in a play-pen, crawling over each other, dribbling and emitting their world-saluting noises. 'Finish your washing,' Rhonwen said, noticing a soaking load of nappies and two or three already wrung out in a bowl alongside the sink.

'I was just going to take all of them to the line before the sun goes. Won't be a minute.'

One of the twins gripped Rhonwen's finger with surprising ferocity. She made the usual addresses to them. Through the window over the sink the father could be seen pegging the nappies on a garden line. It was known in Bedd that he had a passion for washing his twins' nappies, his wife bragging that, because of his gigantic hands, he got them cleaner than she or boiling could.

Back in the kitchen, he thoroughly rinsed the aluminium sink. 'Hannah will be sorry to have missed you. She won't be back until nine. She's gone in Jinny Morgan's car to the early performance in the cinema.'

Rhonwen sat on a hard chair. 'I've just come from Mrs Pyle-Williams,' she began, meditative.

'She wants Hannah to be treasurer of the Women's Guild. Thinks the money will be safe in a police cottage, I expect.' Vaughan beamed at his offspring. 'Noisy geese, aren't they? You would like a cup of tea?'

'I had one with Mrs Pyle-Williams.' Really it was her time for something alcoholic, but she couldn't expect that here. Delaying no more, her handbag on her knees, she continued, 'She wouldn't believe me when I told her I pushed Adda over Pen Mawr cliff. Or that I set fire to Cartref.'

Vaughan did not reach for his tunic, hanging on a door-peg. A minute elapsed before, emerging from depths well beyond his experience, he observed, 'I'm not surprised she wouldn't believe you'. Doubtless he too had heard of the drinking.

'She thinks I ought to go to Brynawel for treatment.' Impatience scudded throughout the blank calm.

Vaughan ran a hand over his neatly tonged waves of hair. Rhonwen's announcements were the stranger because she sat before him with the unruffled response of a woman nipping in to gossip of some ordinary village enterprise. Aware that his intelligence as Bedd's representative of the law might be in peril of censure from his superiors, he protested, 'Accidental death, wasn't it? The Melin police took up the case after I reported your husband's disappearance. I remember they went to interview a lady you met picking blackberries on the day he fell down the cliff.' More decisive, he said, 'And Adda was cremated!' For him it seemed to clinch the matter.

One twin was crying 'Ah, ah, ah,' the other warbling in a lower key. Rhonwen said, 'Even if he'd been buried it wouldn't be any use digging him up. I never tried to poison him.'

Finding a bolt-hole, Vaughan said suddenly, 'Isn't it best for you to see Dr Llewellyn?'

'I set fire to Cartref,' she repeated, certain now that Mrs

Pyle-Williams had telephoned Vaughan with some kind of warning immediately she had left Plas Clynnog.

Vaughan was obliged to consider again, staring out of the window at the nappies quietly flapping in the breezy last sunshine. 'That is not what was decided by the insurance representatives who came down. One man called to see me. Your character in Bedd couldn't be higher. Dan Evans said the same, I know.'

She gave no response to this. 'I'm not going to Brynawel for treatment. Plenty of people need it more than I do.'

Perhaps to divert her from her obsession, he related, nodding, 'Well, lately there's been a little bit of disturbance from a boy of sixteen, but I don't think he's a case for Brynawel. Works on a farm and lives with his mother down beside the river. He chased a girl down a lane one night after a dance in the Memorial Hall and had his way. She's well under sixteen. She ran home screaming at the top of her voice and her mother went to the minister of Salem Chapel for advice. He went to talk to the boy. "Why did you do it?" he asked, and all the boy said was "Because I felt like it". The Rev came to see me, we sat on him, and the Rev went to the boy again. "Borstal or marriage," he told him. "Choose." The girl was willing for marriage, though she had screamed so loud three weeks before. They can live in her mother's front room and between them they'll make a man of him. So the offence has not been reported to me officially. Some things are best hushed up.'

Rhonwen rose to go. 'I am not going to call on the minister of Salem.'

Vaughan glanced at the loud kitchen clock. 'Dr Llewellyn's evening surgery opens at six thirty.'

She felt even more certain that he had been forewarned by Mrs Pyle-Williams. 'You are not going to put what I have told you into your notebook?'

'My head's a good notebook,' he replied, looking unbudging. He might have been accustomed to hundreds of hysterical or warped women making a nuisance of themselves. Truly balanced and kindly himself, now that he had escaped from yieldings to various temptations in London, he ushered his visitor out with the utmost friendliness. 'Everybody remembers,' he reminded her, 'that you rescued Adda's ashes when your house was blazing.

Standing on the lawn with the casket and nothing else!'

She had the last word. 'My expensive fur coat.'

Dr Euros Llewellyn's house was only two minutes' drive. It was a rambling, creeper-dark old dwelling, which had once been a coaching inn. Entrance to the surgery lay in the cobbled side-yard fringed with tumbledown stables. Gwendolyn, now the doctor's wife after a talked-about long period as his receptionist and general helpmate, failed to recognise the trim, smartly-dressed Rhonwen at once. 'For a renewal of prescription is it?' she asked, and, told the caller's name, exclaimed 'I thought you had run off to live in England!'

'I want to see Euros.'

'What's the matter with you?'

'It's private.'

Gwendolyn, who smelt of whisky and underwear, as they stood in a dank airless passage, said, 'Didn't your house go on fire?' She had never joined the Women's Guild, rarely went out and, it was said, wore a circular astrakhan hat in bed during the winter, some declaring they had seen it used as a cosy on a teapot also.

'I set fire to it myself.'

A dog barked loudly. 'Shut up, Mike,' Gwendolyn bawled, and confided, 'He doesn't like evening surgery. Never barks in the morning ones. Now, you want a renewal of prescription? For sleeping tablets, isn't it?'

'I want to see Euros.'

Gwendolyn unwillingly took her into the consulting room, a musty den with a scroll-end sofa, a littered desk, a smudged glass case containing instruments, a cat fast asleep on its top. 'He's got bad lumbago,' she referred to her husband. 'I tell him it's because of this damp old house, but he won't leave it. People think because a house was in history it should be propped up and kept bandaged with safety pins. But it's a bugger to keep clean and warm.' Absently, she added, 'I could set fire to it when I'm worked up.' She went to summon Euros.

He did not appear for several minutes. Aged about seventy-five, he was a man of strict principles, and a faithful deacon of his Baptist chapel since its crowded days. He even disapproved of the Bowling Club in speech, but on the whole was affectionate towards every true native of Bedd; all his own ancestors were buried there. 'Now, what's the matter, Rhonwen?' He squeezed his obese frame into his swivel chair at the desk, a rheumy eye resting guardedly on her where she sat upright on the lumpy sofa, looking anything but a downtrodden widow. 'You've lost a dozen years!' Blondie and Blackie would have preened themselves, justly. 'Want to transfer to another doctor now you're living somewhere else? A bad business for you, Cartref going on fire like that!'

'No, not a bad business. *I* set it on fire.'

'Let me see now . . . how is your sleeping? You've been taking those barbiturates for . . . how long?' The outer doorway tinkled, signalling the arrival of a patient, and Gwendolyn's and a man's voices could be heard.

'I haven't come to complain about not sleeping. I'm sleeping easier since Cartref burned down. It was haunted by a red-horned ram after I pushed Adda over Pen Mawr cliff.'

He gave her three or four seconds' brooding scrutiny, and commented, 'Rhonwen, you haven't got a leg to stand on.'

Mrs Pyle-Williams must have telephoned him. The two shared a passion to keep Bedd unsullied, including not only the preservation of old houses, but the decencies of family life within them. Had the policemen telephoned too? 'I wanted to speak the truth,' Rhonwen said, knees firmly together. 'I've told Mrs Pyle-Williams and Constable Vaughan this afternoon. They won't believe me.'

A sudden gleam of angry reproof came into his gaze, as the outer door-bell tinkled again and the dog barked. 'Nobody would believe you! You are deceiving yourself too. I am a busy doctor concerned with troubles of the body. But I can arrange for you to see a psychiatric consultant at Brynawel if you wish.'

'No.'

Deeper testiness caused his body to heave. 'The self-deceit of people! Hallucinations, in advanced cases. People come here whining, hypochondriacs imagining illnesses and other fancies, and I send them packing with a prescription for sedatives or a bottle of foolish medicine.' He shook a finger at her. 'But most of them are not cases for Brynawel.'

'I am not either.'

'What makes you go about saying these things now, against all reason and the verdict of an inquest and findings of Dan Evans's insurance firm?'

'For my peace of mind I want to speak the truth.'

'You don't stop to think you're making yourself a damned annoyance to people? Limelight, attention — that's what you are after, Rhonwen?' His indignant eyes swept over her clothes, her deftly preserved face, the high-class achievement of her hair, and he banged his fist on the desk. 'What proof have you got that you pushed Adda over a cliff and set fire to Cartref? What would you think if Jane Pyle-Williams went about saying she had poisoned her two husbands? Lay off the bottle, Rhonwen, or you might end by having serious d.t.'s and be taken to Brynawel forcibly! Take another think about yourself. If you want me to arrange a consultation at Brynawel, phone me. Now, off with you. How many sleeping tablets are left from your last prescription?'

She sat passive now. 'Only five or six. I was going to ask you for a renewal while I'm here.'

He jotted on a leaf of his pad and handed it to her. 'Only twenty-five for you this time, not a hundred.'

'Why?'

'Because you are temporarily unbalanced.'

She put the leaf in her bag without protest and rose. 'They still bring dreams, but the red-horned ram never comes now.' She stroked the head of the wakened cat; Euros opened the door for her and shouted 'Next' down the passage, where three people sat on a long bench. She said to him, 'I feel better already. But I will be changing my doctor.'

She had done it! Confession, almost in full, had been made to three representatives of social life in Bedd, not counting Insurance Evans. She had decided not to reveal Eirene as the reason for her punishing Adda, its details of the purchase of a house, the cheque-book stubs disclosing other expenditures, and, most potent of all, the fury of a spurned wife. Such revelation might cause the wrecking of another life, and Eirene was not an evil woman. Even Alcwyn might be affected by the ruin; Eirene might lose her non-legal guardianship of the boy. The punitive force for disreputable conduct made public was roused to its most mischievous and destructive pitch when sex was concerned.

She had done it! Driving down the long valley, the enclosing mountains sitting on both sides with such assurance of protection, she felt she was inside a clear sphere of light. Nobody could reach her there. The sphere was hard as crystal. Sometimes she had wondered about those mysterious confession boxes in Roman Catholic churches; dark, secret, and even forbidding though they looked, did a wrongdoer emerge from them into a clear dazzle of light, really purged of dross? Oh, she had done it. Exorcism was almost completed. Would she be clapped into prison if she allowed the compulsion to self-accusation to persist? No. Somehow she had known she would not be believed. She stopped the car a few yards from the turning into a quiet side road, a short distance up which stood the Druid's Chair, a cosy pub not much patronized except by farmers, shepherds and the odd visitor to a few supposed prehistoric remains in the vicinity. Her mouth was dry. The now familiar need to obliterate loneliness began to gnaw at her, within the clear sphere of light. Yet it did not possess its former irresponsible dictation. She drove past the turning with sudden resolution. It was miraculous that the exalted resolution was maintained for the rest of that evening, and she went to bed early, allowing herself two sleeping tablets.

In the morning she took, for the first time, a new four-hour treatment instituted by Blondie and Blackie in their enlarged premises. In addition to the normal hair-styling, shampoo and set and a facial, there was now body massage on a plain hard board like a carpenter's trestle table, given in a back room marked *Private*, its door also guarded by a gaudily painted wood statue of a turbaned young blackamoor. The fee was ten pounds, inclusive of coffee or tea, prim triangular sandwiches and tiny pastries. Blondie, reputed to be Swedish-trained and certificated, was the masseur, and an ordeal of complete nudity was expected from the customers, though briefs could be worn if insisted upon. That the renovated customer, on leaving, was presented with a rose, carnation or other flower from Blodwen's nearby florist shop lifted the whole operation into a poetic domain. It was said that several farmers' wives from remote fastnesses, some with prosperous

Thursday market stalls in Melin, were on a waiting list for the treatment. Rhonwen, as a regular patron and a credit to the establishment, could always get priority, as she did for the four-hour labouring on her that morning.

In the afternoon she took her hothouse rose downstairs to Eirene. Her landlady willingly stopped typing to take an early cup of tea with her, an hour before Alcwyn would arrive from school, and she had listened to Rhonwen's confession with attention, not speaking or betraying shock as the short, unemotional recital proceeded. Her cup of tea finished, she sat twirling the rose, allowing herself half a cigarette, stubbed out earlier.

'Now, Rhonwen, you only *thought* you pushed him over Pen Mawr. Most people want to do such things at some time or other — the impulse comes, and goes as fast as it came. Or we dream such things at night, when there's too many blankets on the bed or we've eaten something wrong.' A compassionate glance at the woman in the rocking chair carried reservations. 'It's my belief that you *thought* you set fire to Cartref too. A red-horned ram haunting the house speaks for itself. Imagination!' At the back of her mind was memory of the route to Brynawel, the route taken by Alcwyn's mother, its preliminaries familiar to her. 'We women, we can go off our rocker about so many things!' Realizing that Rhonwen actually occupied a rocking chair, she laughed. 'Oh, Rhonwen!'

'You don't believe me, then?'

'I do *not*. Rhonwen, it's the drink and depression. I'm ashamed to see so many bottles in our rubbish bin on Wednesdays — they must make the collecting men think. Have you ever seen coloured snakes running about the bottom of your bed?'

'No. There was only the ram in Cartref — and he came before I began to drink the bottles Dan Evans had ordered for Adda's funeral, in case people would be at the house afterwards.' With the same precision, Rhonwen continued, 'When I drove away in the car after Adda went over Pen Mawr and the seagulls were screaming, I saw a red-horned ram staring at me from a clump of bushes close to the cliff top — the one that came to haunt me in Cartref.' She finished, 'He never comes here. So it isn't drink that brings him.' The logic seemed infallible.

'You had the sense to increase the insured value of Cartref before you set fire to it,' Eirene remarked thoughtfully.

'Dan Evans suggested it. There's no connection between that and the fire.'

'Rhonwen,' Eirene declared, briskly for her, 'our minds slip and then shift back to true balance again. Full of sly tricks beyond our control sometimes, especially in women. Long before she was taken to Brynawel, Alcwyn's mother had slips only in the middle of the week, when she was worried over money — until she became . . . *advanced*.'

'I'm not mad.' Rhonwen began to rock the chair in a slow rhythm. 'It's been a strain to keep to myself, that's all.'

'Nobody will believe a word of it.' Eirene spoke with emphatic conviction. 'At least,' she amended, 'not about you pushing Adda over the cliff. No doubt some people set fire to their houses or business premises, but that's a small matter compared to doing away with a husband. Besides, if you had done it I don't think you would blab about it.'

'It was the ram made me set fire to Cartref,' Rhonwen persisted. 'True, the extra insurance money was welcome . . . . In the old days,' she mused, 'widows used to be put in almshouses.'

'That was long before the days of Blondie and Blackie!' At this taunt, Rhonwen even smiled, and Eirene proceeded, 'I don't think you ought to keep Adda's ashes upstairs under your eyes all day.'

'The lid fits tight and is locked with a tiny key. That box cost fourteen pounds and I didn't begrudge a penny of it. The tin urn they sold me at the crematorium was common and in bad taste, and I put it in the garage at Cartref until I could decide what to do with the ashes.'

'Ashes are nothing.'

'You weren't Adda's wife. I thought I would send them to our daughter in Australia, but now I've decided that she doesn't deserve them.' Rhonwen's jaw, as sometimes happened, jutted out of its normal abeyance, and her lips, a carmine seal, closed into a tight blob. All the lower part of her face, usually the most revealing outward feature of the mystery of a person's inner sanctum, where everybody is alone, set into a daunting hardness, until the conversation was resumed.

Eirene murmured, from her own reverie, 'Men wreck us women. That silly carrot they've got has done more mischief than politics, the big guns of war or religion. A man seems to think it's his own property and he can do what he likes with it, beholden to nobody and nothing.'

Rhonwen followed her own disjointed train of thought. 'I'm sure Adda wasn't liked in the Bowling Club. He provoked people. Bumptious, full of himself, conceited.' She ran on more obsessively. 'Then his meanness. The sixty-watt light bulbs in Cartref made me want to push one down his throat. Meanness, meanness. He was generous to you, but that meant generosity to himself. Dodging the expense of us going to Australia to see our daughter! He didn't know, as I know now, that Marged wouldn't cry her eyes out if we didn't go. Not long before he died I changed the sixty-watt bulb in our bedroom to a hundred-and-fifty one. The next night, I went to bed long after him, switched on the light, and it was the sixty-watt there again. He was fast asleep, with his back to my place, and I looked at his face and saw him dead. He had done the same when I changed the living room bulb. They call it the last straw. But it wasn't. On our last trip to Pen Mawr he drove the car down this street, out of our route, and he looked at this house. It strengthened my mind, and everything went beautifully that afternoon. Not a soul up there, and no boat on the water.'

His lover made no attempt to defend him or to be more convinced by these avowals. She had decided, that all Rhonwen's mental upheaval had its beginning in Adda's conjugal unfaithfulness. Rhonwen had been reared in the strict old chapel-order of living, and try as she might to change herself with beauty treatments, show-off clothes and drink, traces of the hoary puritanism remained deeply embedded. Stoicism helped Eirene now. Rhonwen's presence in the house would not bring alarm deriving from this afternoon's strange so-called confession. Escape from her bitter crisis seemed to be indicated. How kind and affectionate she was to Alcwyn! Judging by her concern over him he would never be in want while she was alive. She had mentioned that he should go to a college later, Llandovery or Lampeter.

'You won't see a psychiatrist at Brynawel, as you said the doctor suggested yesterday?'

'No.'

Eirene's tear ducts burst. Dabbing with tissue, she said, without any evidence of grief, 'Sometimes I think I ought to see a psychiatrist myself. Could he tell me why I don't want to marry any man? Dewi Dowdall-Jones sent me English sonnets to type the other day, and I'm sure he was making a proposal to me in them, referring to someone called Niobe crying over her typewriter and lonely at nights in the future when she couldn't work any more. He's too shy and backward to bring the matter up when he comes here. But I wouldn't marry him, though he'll have a good pension when he retires from teaching. No poets for me! Businessmen are best — you know where you are with them. But I won't marry anyone, I won't.' She continued, 'Is it because Adda filled me that I don't want to marry? I was seventeen when I first took to him, three or four months after I started work on the Gas Board. He used to drive me to those woods under Clogwyn.' Plunged down her own memory lanes, she added, 'Never mind about that little affair with the cane and one or two other stupid fancies that came later. He filled me, and he gave me this house.'

It was not challenging or bragging, only a statement of ordinary facts, spoken with modesty, and it held an acceptable contrast to the legal wife's freakish delusions. That, vicariously, Eirene also had a child to rear was an additional fulfilment. She was not lonely. Neither was she harassed, although short of ready money on occasion.

Rhonwen brooded for some moments, quietly rocking. Nobody would have judged her a woman racked by secret tumults of guilt and retribution, or a woman gone off her head with imaginings of murder and arson. As though all passion was spent now, neither did she betray the least resentment at Eirene's references to her long association with Adda, from seventeen, when he must have been nearing forty.

She said, 'Why won't people believe I did it? Is that to be my punishment?'

'Perhaps you didn't expect people to believe you?' The widow's chair stopped rocking abruptly, and her exchange of glances with Eirene was like a fusion, a connivance. Eirene continued flatly, 'I still think it was some kind of accident up on Pen Mawr. I dare say that deep down inside you *wanted* to push him over a cliff. We get bouts of hysteria. You were having a nervous breakdown because you had found out about me. A woman that actually pushes her husband over a cliff and then goes picking blackberries to make bramble jelly for him, as you said you did — it doesn't make sense, and I do *not* believe you, punishment though it may be for you.' In her manner lay all the feminine ability to dismiss the impact of unpleasantness, obliterate it by the simple expedient of banging a door against it. She sat contemplating her house-mate with all the indulgence of her inbred charity. Hadn't she understood and forgiven Rhonwen's threats to obtain ownership of the house and also back-rent from her and Alcwyn's father? In turn, hadn't Rhonwen taken her to Torquay?

'They don't even ask me *why* I did it,' Rhonwen said, still musing.

'Well, *I* am asking you.' Eirene spoke patiently, as one might to a fractious child.

'There was a time when I had power over him. Then I lost it. If if hadn't been you as a cause it would have been another girl. That requires kneeling to, and I couldn't do it — I see my mistake now, when it's too late. When I found out about you I ought to have taken a lover myself. But I was too old and, besides, besides, it would have gone against the grain with me, against what a wife feels for her husband of a lifetime and keeps her spine straight.' Since Eirene said nothing, she repeated, 'That day when we went to Pen Mawr he drove the car out of our way just to go past your house — I already knew your address. It made my blood boil.'

Eirene allowed herself some self-justification, weak though it was — 'Adda ran after me, not me after him. I didn't raise a finger to *keep* him running after me either.'

'I had decided that was true. It is why I came here to live with you and Alcwyn.' Rhonwen added, 'I have never told anyone about you and Adda.'

Eirene rose and stood looking out of the window for a minute or two of heavy thought, which in her meant ninety per cent feeling and emotion. When she turned to look at Rhonwen there was a mystical heightening in her manner as she said, 'You must have the deeds of this house transferred to you.'

'No.' The reply could not have come quicker.

'He meant more to you even than to me. He would never have given me a nervous breakdown. Take the deeds please, Rhonwen.'

'Never.'

'Not if I died?'

'Why do you say that?' Rhonwen was attendant to significance weighing the air. 'You're over twenty years younger than I am.'

'What if there's something the matter with my heart, same as with my tear ducts? Years are not the point; anything can happen this year, next year. I'm going to make a will tomorrow! I had thought of it in bed a week or two ago — you've worried me and made me feel bad. This house will be left to you, and if you die before me, to Alcwyn. A hundred pounds to my sister up in Pwll.' She looked at her watch. 'It isn't too late to phone the Solicitor's office. He has sent typing jobs to me when his secretary's been on holiday.' She took up her address book and the phone receiver, chatted sociably to someone, fixed an appointment for early the next morning, before the magistrates' court opened, and laid the receiver down. 'Tomorrow morning at nine sharp. You can't stop me doing that.' All at once she had attained a degree of authority, even ascendancy. 'I must put things straight while I've got health and a sound head.'

Rhonwen, also roused, got up from her chair at once. 'I'm with the other solicitor in Melin, Madoc Howells.' She found his number in the directory. An appointment for the next afternoon was fixed. She laid down the receiver casually. 'I will have a new will drawn up. My estate will be divided into equal shares for three persons — you, Alcwyn, and my daughter in Australia who doesn't want me. Marged was left everything in my previous will.'

Eirene's automatic protests were of no avail. The arrival of Alcwyn, who had been given his father's front door key, interrupted the discussion. If he could have known that it had just been decided to allocate him, barring changes, a nice sum of money, he might not have angrily flung his satchel to the floor and shouted. 'You haven't laid my tea! I'm hungry, what's the matter?' Did he sense a portentousness in the air? 'Someone has died?' His nostrils quivered. 'There's something smelling.' A faint odour of vinegar and onions permeated the ground floor. A casserole of herrings was sousing at a slow heat in Eirene's new cooker, changed from gas to electricity when her kitchen was redecorated the previous week.

Alcwyn's surrogate mother bustled and his honorary aunt interested him in an account of her morning's invigorating massage at Blondie and Blackie's. After tea he ran out to inspect the Angora rabbit given to a neighbour's son who had returned from an operation at Melin hospital, and in the resumed conversation Eirene was not given an inkling of the current extent of her benefactress's capital. 'Well, thank you very much,' she finally closed the subject. 'I always thought I wouldn't die a starved old maid.'

As it was likely that Rhonwen would die long before her, she had done quite well for herself, possession of the disputed house remaining hers. Even before that day renovation, a clearing-up, lay in her ambience. She had begun to bloom with it after Alcwyn's father was harassed out of the house. Possession of Alcwyn, although precarious legally, added to her air of liberation. The air was infectious. Rhonwen's abstinence from drink, a gradual process, began from this time. Confession of her misdeed, though not accepted, aided her. The crystal sphere enclosing her remained intact. Upstairs that evening she drank two glasses of sherry, took a walk when impulse for more bothered her, and arrived back at eight o'clock for the soused herrings which, cooled by then, she had been invited to share. Sharing of company and domesticity, including overseership of a small boy, were other aids to forgetfulness.

The next day, both women returned from their respective solicitor's office with a photostat copy of their simple wills, and also with the look of satisfaction such as an important activity can provide. The original copies remained with the solicitors. Both exchanged their copies for reading over an early cup of tea and a round jam sponge cake bought by Rhonwen on her way back from Madoc Howells' office. 'Mr Howells did not tear up the old will,' she remarked. 'But the date of today's one cancels it and says previous wills are revoked.' They soon talked of something else. Conversation on the subject of one's will is often evanescent as sunsets. Only a corpse brings them to vivid and prolonged life.

Rhonwen left the house before Alcwyn arrived from school. She carried a shopping bag of limp black leatherette. Eirene, singing at work in the kitchen, did not see or hear her go.

She drove a little way beyond the town and got out of the car in a deserted lane running down to the audible river. A footpath wound among bracken and reeds besides the boulder-strewn water which here, in the hilly Melin district, was at its most talkative, dashing, falling and eddying with various resonances, like so many rivers in Wales and perhaps one of the tonal origins of the melodious language. There were flashing blue and white flingings of pure mountain water, miniature falls and, here and there, sudden deep pools of ambling azure, some close to the low bank.

She found a convenient spot, knelt, and took out of the shopping bag a gilded box, already unlocked at home. The quietly swirling water a few inches below her was so clear that pebbles gleamed blue and grey in the depths. She emptied the gritty contents of the box into this murmuring wash. They did not sink into the moving water; they were swept away at once, towards the turbulent, rocky middle of the river. She felt no particular emotion, except a flickering renewal of the sense of deliverance that had come to her since her confession to five people, who chose not to believe her.

Back at home, she dusted the interior of the box and fetched from the small, makeshift kitchen constructed when the house was divided into two flats a plastic white bag printed with the name of a thriving Melin supermarket. She emptied its contents into the erstwhile urn. They were trading stamps given by the supermarket, to be exchanged for gifts. Eirene, who couldn't be bothered to accumulate hers, always gave them to Rhonwen, who needed three thousand points for a wristwatch for Alcwyn, his first. Then she baked a custard made from the rich local milk and five free-range eggs bought from a farmer's daughter at her market stall.

She took no drink at all that evening. To ease the hankering at her customary hour, she went downstairs with the nutmeg-sprinkled custard. It was a favourite dish of Alcwyn's. Eirene was typing. Alcwyn sat at the window table in the lingering rosy light, busy with his watercolours. Eirene thought he would grow out of his mania for painting and favoured his craving to drive a car. But painting kept him quiet. Absorbed, his face was hidden by his sheaves of hair.

Eirene stopped work and beamed at the custard. 'You went out. I heard you driving back in the car.'

Rhonwen sat as usual in the rocking chair. The craving for a drink was already gone. 'I went down to the river and emptied what was in the golden box I kept locked on my sideboard.'

Alcwyn unexpectedly lifted his head. 'What was in it?' He had wanted to know its contents before and been told not to be inquisitive.

'Go on with your painting.' Eirene commanded. 'Auntie Rhonwen has brought us that lovely custard she knows how to make.' He returned to work, stroking his brush on a vermilion oblong.

'They've reached the ocean by now, I expect.'

Eirene was equally detached. 'We're having steamed hake and parsley sauce tonight. There's enough for three.' She doted on fish.

They talked of cookery. Rhonwen said again how much she missed her old pair of brass scales, lost in the Cartref fire. Presently Dewi Dowdall-Jones called to collect some poems, dropped in on his way to school that morning. Rhonwen always liked his pinched, saturnine face and isolated air, both of which belonged to a man who took life seriously. He flicked over the typed pages, discovered a missing comma instantly. Rhonwen, liking too his dark-tinged voice, asked him to read one of his poems, pleasing him. In English and called 'Sunflower', it was a long thin stem of four-word lines suddenly bursting into a dishevelled cluster of bigger phrases, rhetorical and opulent.

Rhonwen nodded approval. 'I was sorry to hear from Eirene you didn't win the Crown at the Eisteddfod this year,' she said. 'You will one year, you will!'

'Oh, and his poem was first class!' Eirene added comfort.

'Eirene, you can't speak or read Welsh sufficiently to judge,' Dewi pointed out, in his honest way.

She placed her plump little hands over her midriff. 'I felt it was first class down here,' she declared. 'You must keep on, Dewi, keep on. We must never give up doing what gives us pleasure.'

'I don't give it up,' he said grimly. 'How much do I owe you for this lot?'

'One pound, cash down. Ten per cent for credit, as usual.' Eirene switched on a lamp on Alcwyn's table.

It was cash down on this occasion. Magazines in Wales, kept floating on difficult waters by Arts Council aid, printed his work. But the itch to sit robed and crowned on a bardic throne, trumpets blowing and a sword sheathed above his head, on a platform before thousands of enthusiastic non-readers, would always remain, a rash that still might find healing, since his Welsh and technique were perfect, whatever the poetic merit of the content.

A few minutes later, silent Alcwyn rose from his table and deferentially exhibited to the three a page of his sketch book. It displayed an explosive sunflower, its wild petals yellow as his hair, its tense green stalk drawn without wobbling, reaching potently to emit its glory. The painter's work, quick with crude vitality, was of course praised by the three adults. Alcwyn tore out the cartridge sheet and presented it to the poet, who did not teach at his school, so there was no question of calculation.

'I will have it framed, Alcwyn,' Dewi promised, touched by the tribute. 'Now, what can I do for you in return?'

'Turnballs Circus is coming to Bran Field next week. It's my birthday on the Saturday. I'm nine.'

Eirene opened her mouth to a surprised width, and decided not to speak. Dewi said he would take the boy to the afternoon performance. Then Rhonwen herself acknowledged the birthday event, lie though it was, both in date and age.

'Will you all go to lunch with me at Careg Castle on the next day?'

'Merlyn Jenkins' father and mother took him there on a Sunday night,' Alcwyn declared. 'He's been bragging about it — said he saw the ghost they've got, sitting in a hooded chair by the dark stairs, a dog looking up at her and a sword sticking out of her chest.'

'I expect it's a waxwork they've put there to please the tourists,' Dewi said. There was a legend that an erring mistress of the castle had indeed been murdered, her dog whining, off and on, for centuries afterwards.

A visit to Careg Castle had become for some well-off local

people a necessary event. The residence of the late Sir Idwal Prys had been opened as an expensive restaurant, with a few bedrooms available to approved persons. The venture found glossy publicity in English papers. A pair of young men from London ran it, one a retreated West End actor, and both of them bosom friends of Blondie and Blackie. The reputation of their food and elegant decor was so high that long-snouted cars from distant parts made for the victuals and, rain allowing, a stroll in the famous park, with its deer, peacocks and lake in which an international dolphin had been installed by the enterprising young men, whose financial backing remained obscure.

Rhonwen's invitation had been accepted, Eirene pleased at this opportunity to wear a new dress bought during this revivification period she too was undergoing. 'Dewi,' Rhonwen said, 'I forgot to tell Mrs Pyle-Williams when I saw her the other day that you might be persuaded to give another talk to the Women's Guild. I could ask her to come to our lunch at Careg Castle.' He and Eirene consented, and Rhonwen telephoned Plas Clynnog at once. But at the mention of taking a meal at the castle the president exploded, her voice audible in the room.

'No, I will not enter Careg Castle while those Arabs or whatever they are own it. A disgrace to our country. Whatever's the matter with you, Rhonwen? Have you arranged to see the psychiatrist at Brynawel yet?'

'I don't intend to. I'm only asking you to take lunch with my friends, including Dewi Dowdall-Jones, the poet who writes beautifully in Welsh and will be winning the Crown or Chair in the National one year.'

Mrs Pyle-Williams was heedless of this opportunity for cultural patronage. 'These foreigners come here with their money, make more, and then clear off sharp as foxes, same as the wicked coal-barons and iron-kings in the old days hopped from Glamorgan as soon as their fortunes were made and coal began to drop in demand. I've been told that Ceinwen Philips often goes to Careg Castle to play her harp and sing our sweet old songs, sitting in national costume during a meal. If I saw her there I'd bang her tall black hat down over her face. I'm keeping an eye open for her when I go to Melin market on Thursdays, and she'll get a dressing-down, I can tell you! A Judas member of Plaid Cymru. She gets paid ten pounds, sitting there in her check flannel skirt and red shawl among a lot of guzzling traitors and foreigners, in a castle where one of the truest old families in our land kept things pure. When Sir Idwal died and there was no ready cash left for his dear Welsh-speaking wife, only that harmless castle and the park, I wanted the place to be preserved as a conference centre or memorial college or something. I helped to form a committee, until people went off the boil about it. I won't have a penny of my money put into the pockets of that couple of scheming cooks there. Sir Idwal and Lady Charlotte must be turning in the grave they're sharing. I —'

'It will be my money for lunch,' Rhonwen halted her.

'Then you've got more money than feeling. Walk into the kitchen and pour a pan of soup over the heads of those thieving cooks.' The president's receiver was put down with a bang.

'I'll speak to her another time about your talk,' Rhonwen told Dewi. 'Now and again she lets a swarm of nationalist bees into her bonnet.'

Dewi spoke with some approval. 'Is it true that she's one of those people who go out in the middle of the night with paint and blacken English place-names from road sign-posts?'

'I don't know. But she would help pay the expenses for it.'

'You've got to do provoking things and make banging noises to make headway in such campaigns as nationalism,' Dewi said. 'Plaid Cymru and the Welsh Language Society are fighting face-less powers that can't stop to care if the campaign is to keep Wales innocent and dewy.'

Eirene said, 'The country is too old to have dew on it any more, Dewi.'

'A lot of Welsh people like to walk backwards into the past,' Rhonwen contributed. 'Mrs Pyle-Williams and her lot want to build another kind of Offa's Dyke. But you can't keep out all the English industrialists who will provide work or the people who will come here with them and seldom want to learn the Welsh language.'

'Wales is schizophrenic and too minor and low in population to cure that,' Dewi said. 'But we must admire and support all the

Mr and Mrs Pyle-Williamses who shake their fists this side of Offa's Dyke.'

Rhonwen gazed at him pensively along her neat, pure-curved nose. He was so secret and retreated into a melancholy self. There was something padlocked, chained, bolted and barred in him. He retained — as she had as a young woman, and had thought herself coupled safely to a man — much of the stubborn heritage of thou-shalt-not puritanism, the manufactory of extreme suspicion of pleasure, the bleak parsimony that a conquered nation had endured over hundreds of years, reaching extreme obduracy in the nineteenth century and still persisting in less frozen forms. True, Dewi escaped into writing poetry, found degrees of pleasure on that high plateau. It had become all that really mattered to him. She understood Eirene's drawing back from his half-hearted solicitations for marriage. Eirene was too carnal and he too under-weighted with it. A poem written to her would give her pleasure and last no longer than a sprig of mignonette. Adda had given her a house.

He left with his scripts of five English poems. After the occupants of the house had eaten the Milford Haven hake and the baked custard, and Alcwyn was sent off to bed in his small room that had once been an all-glass conservatory, Rhonwen fetched her knitting down. Eirene was finishing typing menu cards for Sian's little daytime restaurant. This sitting together downstairs had become a frequent occurrence. It deepened the concord between the two women.

'I know all Sian's lunch dishes like I know the Lord's Prayer, but on most days she decides to give her customers a special treat. It's stuffed lambs' hearts tomorrow.'

'Why doesn't she write her menus?' Rhonwen knitted peaceably. The rose-shaded light shone from the window table; another at the desk was peach-tinted. Not a sound came from the well-kept street of traditional houses.

'She can't spell. I wouldn't be surprised she can't write English, either. But her cooking crowds that poky restaurant behind the Market. She phones me and says "Just the same dozen cards for Wednesday, except that I'll be giving them *cawl*." The last thin card was done. 'There!' Opening a half-pound box of chocolates, given her by a neighbour for typing a business letter, Eirene sat down opposite Rhonwen in the worn lounge chair she favoured. 'Alcwyn will like that white sweater you're doing ready for the winter.'

Rhonwen accepted a chocolate tipped with a violet petal. Her smile was that of a doting aunt who was much more often a good woman than otherwise. 'Telling lies to Dewi about his birthday, so that he could go to the circus!'

Eirene bit into a ginger-centred chocolate. 'We all tell lies.'

'Yes, we can't go on living comfortably or safely without them.'

Munching, Eirene watched her knitting housemate in the speculative way which occasionally would glaze her eyes, so apt to weep. But Rhonwen's face seldom revealed anything of consequence. Sometimes there was a quick rigidity of her eyelids, in unison with an unattractive hardening of the lower part of her face, as though some mysterious hidden ferocity exhibited itself momentarily, something primitive that would not find true verbal expression, only a counterfeit. These rare glimpses could make Eirene's wandering attention pause, despite the refusals in her nature to allow power to the bad things in life. But no gospel revelation came to her.

She said, 'I'm glad those ashes are out of the house. I never liked to think of them upstairs.'

'Yes. I believe it's going to help me not to drink.'

Eirene took a walnut-topped chocolate. 'It's made me remember what Sarah Thomas did with her husband's ashes. My sister up in Pwll is a neighbour of hers. Sarah kept the casket at home for a week, then one fine night when everybody was in bed she went out and scattered the ashes over the front doorstep of the Cambrian pub. Early next morning she told people what she'd done — "It was where he was happiest," she explained. The pub was one of the old kind that don't encourage women to go in. Husbands sitting there night after night, leaving their wives lonely at home. I couldn't blame Sarah for making a stand like that. She said she couldn't afford proper clothes because of all the money her Dai spent in Cambrian, couldn't take a holiday in Llandudno.'

'What happened to the ashes on the doorstep?'

'I'm coming to that. News about it spread fast and of course people went to look. The ashes were still there, the summer night being dry and no wind. The pub doesn't open till half past ten and when the landlord unbolted his front door there were two or three elderly regulars standing beyond the step, waiting to tell him what Sarah had done. But the coward wouldn't sweep the ashes away. He phoned the police and they said they had no power to act in such a matter. More old regulars arrived but they wouldn't tread on the wide step, only a younger one who was able to leap over it — the others went in by the private side door. Then someone said he'd sweep up the ashes for a double scotch. He used a dustpan and brush and tipped them over the old railway embankment behind the pub.'

'His wife couldn't have had much feeling for him,' Rhonwen observed, accepting another chocolate.

'Or too much?' Eirene questioned, and resumed, 'It wasn't the end of that affair. The landlord said his business began to go down from then and Sarah was a witch and had laid a curse on his pub. She's no more a witch than I am. Opinion was that men would think of their own end when they trod across that big stone step to go in where they used to enjoy themselves, safe and free together, as they had thought. Anyway, business in a pub in the next street began to go up, so there could have been a curse from Sarah. Behind her back up in Pwll she's nicknamed Sarah the Ashes.'

'That woman showed bad taste,' Rhonwen commented. 'Bad taste and courage.' She rolled up the completed front piece of Alcwyn's sweater and stabbed her needles into a ball of wool woven in the reawakened old mill beside the turbulent river. 'Yes, courage. Men take us too much for granted.'

'Oh, but we've got great power over them,' Eirene said earnestly. 'It's a power lying in our private little cave.' A mystical, far-away look came to her face; she might have been visited by atavistic stirrings of primitive rituals never to be done away with, only changed by moral attitudes to them.

After a silence, Rhonwen said, hands relaxed on her lap, 'Adda was beating *me* with that cane he used on you. The savage that always wants to be free needed recognition and satisfaction.'

First, Eirene said, 'Well, I told you the lashes weren't hard,' then, more reflectively, almost pleadingly, 'perhaps some men show their love that way?'

'That's far-fetched.'

'Things in them often are . . . we mustn't allow them to get full control of our feelings, that's all. We can get downtrodden too easily. There's less of that today, of course.'

'I was downtrodden. By love of him. Then he did not want it, and I retaliated.' Rhonwen prepared to return upstairs.

Eirene did not ask what she meant by 'retaliation'. For her the crucial subject was done with. She would never encourage self-indulgence in quiet, whatever its cause. Should Rhonwen be driven to take treatment at Brynawel asylum for delusions, that could be dealt with when and if it came. To her, Rhonwen seemed to be well on the way to recovery from a dislocation of senses caused by shocks. It did not occur to her that she, the initial culprit, had helped to bring recovery. The wife was as welcome in the house as the husband had been. Misdoing lost its importance as time trod it into the earth.

# Biographical Notes

Rhys Davies was born around the turn of the century in Clydach Vale in the Rhondda Valley, the son of the village grocer. In his early twenties he went to live in London where he became a full-time writer and spent most of the rest of his life. He published sixteen novels durning his lifetime, beginning with *The Withered Root* in 1927, as well as numerous short stories, a play, a successful musical, topographical essays, and an autobiography. He died in 1978. *Ram With Red Horns*, his last novel, is published here for the first time. It will be followed in 1997 by the reprint of his autobiography, *Print of a Hare's Foot.*

Philippa Davies lectures in History for the University of Wales, Aberystwyth and for Coleg Powys, Brecon. Her doctoral research, conducted at the University of Wales, Cardiff, explores the usefulness of imaginative writing to the historian. For its perceptive insights and oblique perspective of Welsh life in the first half of the twentieth century Rhys Davies' considerable literary output has been a central concern.